THE LUST LIST: DEVON STONE

FOUR LETTERS

MIRA BAILEE

NoMi Press

Copyright © 2015 by Mira Bailee
Cover design by Qamber Designs
Editing by Nicole Bailey, Proof Before You Publish

Euphoria Publishing
NoMi Press
www.euphoriapublishing.com

Publisher's Note: This is a work of fiction. Names, characters, places, and incidents are a product of the author's imagination, and any resemblance to actual people, living or dead, or to businesses, companies, events, institutions, or locales is completely coincidental.

ISBN-13: 978-0692420621
ISBN-10: 0692420622

Printed in the United States of America

For Nova,

Couldn't have done this without

you, Hayley, and Kaidan

PROLOGUE

Devon

Nothing better than speeding down a highway after spontaneous, semi-public sex. Never mind the fact the drunk girl I'm driving home isn't my girlfriend.

Heh, *girlfriend.* I'm getting used to the sound of that. Olivia's not like any of the others—thank-fucking-god. Kennedy, Brooke, Layla, the one with the tongue ring and hot-ass side tattoo—what was her name again?

It doesn't matter. I think—and shoot me if I admit this to anyone out loud—I think Olivia could be the real thing. She's got a spunky side, and I can trust her.

Her roommate, Maddie, groans in the passenger seat. She's hunched over, leaning her forehead on my dashboard.

"You gonna make it?" I ask. Girl needs to learn her own boundaries with alcohol, and I'm going to be pissed if she pukes all over the leather interior. People aren't allowed to drive my Camaro, let alone desecrate it with vomit.

"I'm fine," Maddie says, leaning back into the seat and closing her eyes. "Can you slow down? You drive like an ass."

"I'm doing you a favor. You know that right?"

"And I appreciate it, but please," she rubs her temples and exhales loudly, "drive like less of an ass."

"You're nicer when you're sober."

"You probably are too."

What's that supposed to mean? I barely drank tonight, hence the reason I'm the one tasked with getting Maddie home so Olivia can enjoy the rest of the gala. Is she talking about the drugs? Did Olivia tell her?

Clenching my jaw shut to avoid an argument, I press harder on the accelerator. No offense ladies, but neither of you can possibly know what I've been going through. If I knew how to explain it to Olivia, I would, but if her best friend is going to jump down my throat? No thanks.

"She's in love with you, you know," Maddie slurs.

I almost swerve the car into a guard rail at the sound of the "L" word. "Yeah right. We haven't known each other long enough to..." I look over. Maddie's eyes are closed. It's no use discussing it with her. "Trust me," I say quieter to myself, "I wish it were that easy."

"Just tell her," Maddie mumbles.

Fuck. I thought she was passed out. "She wants me to work on myself. I'm trying. No need to complicate it more with...other promises."

No response from my drunk passenger.

"Hey," I say again.

Still quiet. I cough loudly.

Definitely passed out now.

I grip the steering wheel tighter, focusing on the road. The shaking in my hands is getting worse. This is the longest I've gone without some sort of fix. The coke, the pills. Hell, even liquor's acted as my vice for years. And when one girl tells me to stop, I'm supposed to just give it all up?

Not *one* girl. *The* girl.

If it was anyone else telling me what to do, I'd tell them to fuck off.

We pull into Olivia's apartment complex and park. Stopping the car doesn't wake Maddie. Shit, I have to carry her in?

I get out and go to her side, opening the door.

"Hey," I say again, this time nudging her shoulder.

She groans but stays sleeping.

"You're home."

She flings her arm out at me, smacking me in the gut.

Sighing, I reach down for her bag. The keys are probably in here. I find them and warn her, "No more hitting. I'm taking you inside."

I lift her out and help her find her feet. One arm supporting her, the other holding her stuff, we stumble to the door and make our way into the apartment.

Dropping her off in her bed makes me feel more uncomfortable by the second. What the hell do I do in this situation? Tuck her in? Leave her leg dangling off the edge? Being near a woman in a bed usually implies a different scenario—one where Olivia is involved, preferably. This is just...weird.

A quilt hangs on the back of a chair, and I cover her with it. There, I've been the good guy. Now get me out of here.

After I run back out to my car to grab my duffel from the trunk, I go back in to Olivia's room. The quicker I get out of here, the quicker I get my beautiful woman into my penthouse for an unforgettable night. I toss the bag onto her bed and take a look around.

Yeah...I should've asked her what she'd need.

Going a night without anything is easy for me—well, just about anything. I look at my hands again. Still shaking. I hate this bullshit. The jittery feeling. The headaches. The way everything feels like it's going to hell. One thing could fix it.

I shake away the thought. Let's start in the closet. Olivia needs something for tomorrow. Opening it, I scan the options, not knowing a thing about fashion and what goes with what. A little dress catches my attention. It'll show off Olivia's sexy curves, so I grab that and toss it onto the bed. That's it for the closet, yet I can't help but look up at the top shelf before I close the door. Some shoes. And a box.

What's in the box?

How many times have I argued with her for snooping around? And yet... I reach up and grab the box. Just a peek.

Inside are papers, photos, a journal. I flip through the pages, but even I'm not a big enough asshole to invade her privacy so I put it aside. The first photo in the box seems to jump out at me. A teenaged Olivia, dyed black hair with blue streaks. Too much makeup. But the same sexy smile. She's got her arm wrapped around some kid, but it looks forced. I look on the back: *Liv and Jared - J's 14th birthday.*

Shit. It's her brother. The dead one. I can't imagine what it must be like for her. Sure, my own brother's a pain in the ass most of the time, but I'd hate to lose him.

Guilt punches me in the stomach, and I replace everything in the box and stuff it back up in the closet.

What else does she need? Underwear and stuff, right? I move to her dresser and pull open the top drawer. Now *this* is what I like.

Skimpy little thongs and see-through lacy things. This is what dreams are made of. I pick the most revealing one I can find and toss it toward the bed, then find an equally sexy bra. Whether it's functional or fashionable, whatever, I don't know. I'm going with what's hot. If she didn't want to wear it, it wouldn't be in here, I assume.

She has a hairbrush on her dresser, so I add that to the pile. That's got to cover everything. This room smells like her. Sweet, a little floral. It eases my pounding headache and makes me hungry for the taste of her. I have two cravings. Olivia. And cocaine. And fuck my life that the two can't co-exist.

I zip open the duffel, flipping the flap open to toss her things in. My heart stops. This bag hasn't been used since Oregon. Since I'd disappointed Olivia to the point she didn't want to see me again. I was such an asshole up there and should've listened to her. Considered her feelings. It's only sheer luck she didn't ditch me for good.

But this is why I almost blew it.

I reach down and lift out the only thing I'd left in this bag. A little blue tin. The answer to all my problems. My stash.

Inside, a little bag of white powder seduces me. It's as beautiful as... as... no. *Forget about all this shit, Devon. Come on, man.*

I lift out a small pill bottle, shaking it and watching the assortment of pharmaceuticals dance inside the amber-colored plastic. My pulse races. I feel energized. Just one of these.

Just one line to snort.

Just one.

And I'd feel better.

"Fuck." I slam the lid shut on the tin and thrust the thing down into a side pocket. I run my hands through my hair, yanking at the roots. *Fuck.* I can't do this. Throwing Olivia's things into the duffel, I let out a frustrated growl, zip the bag closed, and leave her room, slamming the door behind me.

Is she worth all this trouble?

I stop at the bathroom intending to grab her toothbrush for her. There are two of them, and I don't know which is hers. Never mind. We have brand new, unopened ones in the penthouse. I smile at the reason behind that. Once, I'd gone on a magnificent fucking binge. A one-night stand every night for two weeks. I learned fast to keep the penthouse well-stocked with the essentials. The girls seemed to appreciate it.

And now, look at me. Letting one woman turn my life upside down.

Is she worth it?

I leave the apartment, making sure it's locked when I go.

Fuck yeah, she's worth it.

Driving even faster to get back to the hotel, I battle with the throbbing in my skull. I want to do a line. My mouth wants to swallow a pill. Just one. But more than any drug, I want Olivia.

I toss the keys at the valet as I quickly get out of the car. Grabbing my duffel bag, I jog up to the big double doors. I'm seconds away from devouring my girl. My plan is to get up there, not say a word, and push her on the bed. Our bodies will do the rest.

Olivia's got my key, so I pull out my spare and get the elevator moving. Up and up to my girl. Heart racing, hands shaking. I don't know if it's anticipation or drug withdrawal, but who fucking cares right now? I'll forget all about my addictions in Three. Two. One.

The elevator dings and opens. I rush to my door and unlock it, unable to keep the smile off my face at this point. I waltz in, tossing the bag toward the dining area, and turn toward the bed expecting to find my goddess.

"What the fuck?"

On the bed—correction: *Handcuffed* to the bed, is a woman—if you can call her that—I was ready to kill two years ago. Natasha Vorhees. The craziest stalker I've ever met.

"What the hell are you doing here? Where's Olivia?"

I don't even want to face this chick, but Olivia's nowhere in sight. How'd she get in here? What part of restraining order doesn't she understand?

She's a damn whore on the bed, wearing red lingerie and attached to the headboard with fuzzy black cuffs.

"Don't talk about your girlfriend. Totally kills the mood. Just get over here."

Natasha shifts her legs, spreading them wide. I cringe and turn away. "Like hell I will. Where is she?"

"She's gone. Out of the picture. You're out of excuses, so stop lying to yourself. I'm stuck here and only you can free me." She motions behind me, and I turn and spot the handcuff keys on the floor. What? Did she throw them? And how? With her foot or something? She lowers her eyes and grins a mischievous grin. "I think I can free you too. You look so tense."

"I should've fucking killed you when I had the chance."

Two years ago, she stalked me, threatened my family, and attacked Kennedy— Wait. Where *is* Olivia?

I walk to the side of the bed closest to Natasha's repulsive head. She smiles at me, batting her eyelashes. "I knew you'd give in—"

My hand finds her throat before I can even think to do it. I squeeze her scrawny neck, and her eyes bulge in fear. I lean down close to her ear. "When I let go, you'll tell me what you've been doing to Olivia. You'll tell me where she is. And you'll tell me how you got in this room. Do you understand?"

She gives a slight nod, and I release her.

"Start talking." I fold my arms in front of my chest and work on concealing my worry. One sign of weakness, and this bitch latches on.

"She's too nice. You deserve better."

The closest thing within reach is a small glass vase on a table. I grab it and sling it at the wall just above the headboard. Natasha flinches as water and broken glass rain down around her. "Try again you psychotic bitch."

"It was just too easy, Devon. She's too kind and giving and too caught up in the death of her brother. I got on a bus with her in Oregon. That, and one short meeting, was all I needed to get her working with me. And the more she trusted me, the closer I got to you. Tonight, she was practically groveling at my feet. So I took her hotel key. And I took her place."

"That doesn't make sense. I was with her enough. I would've heard your name. Seen you."

"Oh, did you miss the memo? I go by Natalia now. And as always, I've been one step ahead of you, sweetheart." She shifts on the bed again, running her foot up along the opposite leg. "I know what's best for you. And I know what you want."

I look around. The handcuff keys. I snatch them off the floor and shove them into my pocket. "One step ahead. Right. I'll be back, and this time, your ass is going to jail."

CHAPTER ONE

Olivia

It's so dark. Am I still unconscious?

No. A pounding in my head is getting worse. Stars flash across my vision. It's pitch black, and I'm lying on something metal. How much did I drink tonight? I've never blacked out before.

Natalia. It's all coming back like a slow motion replay. She betrayed me.

She attacked me.

Why?

Devon. She wants Devon.

Oh god. What's she going to do to him? I have to get up.

Move Olivia!

The pain in my head is paralyzing. The rest of my body feels sore and scraped and *buzzing?* There's a buzzing in my chest I can't explain. Rhythmic, matching my inhales. How do heart attacks begin? Is this one?

When my hand touches my chest, the buzzing feels even stronger. Oh wait, it's my phone. I remember I'd stuffed it in my corset before helping Natalia. That lying bitch.

Pulling my phone out, I feel instantly relieved. It's Devon. He's okay.

I hold it to my ear and say hello. At least, I try to say hello.

"Olivia, you there? Where are you?"

Good question. I answer him. Well, I try to answer. Words don't seem to want to come out. "I don't know," I mumble.

The light from the phone illuminates the space around me. When I hold it out, I find I'm in a small storage room. How the hell did I get in here?

Devon's still talking, but I can't concentrate. I need out of here. I need to find him.

"Olivia," I hear him say. He sounds so distant. And so, so angry. "That bitch stole the key card. She went to the penthouse thinking I'd—never mind. You still there?"

I bring the phone back to my ear as I push myself up to standing. "I'm here," I say slowly. My legs wobble, and I grab a ladder to steady my balance.

Using my phone to light the way, I slowly spin, looking for a door. There's a shelf, a wall, another wall. I look at the shelf again. It's open on both sides. I push boxes to the side. Ahh, things make more sense now. Bitch dumped me in the back of this room. The door's around the shelf.

Beep.

Shit. I look at my phone. Devon sounds more frantic. "Olivia. Talk to me. What's wrong? Where are you?"

Beep. My phone's at one percent battery. Not good.

"Devon," I say, still holding my phone out. He can probably hear me. "My phone's about to die. I need the light. Give me a second."

I step over a crate, using the dim light to lead the way. I see a light switch and rush to it. By rush, I mean, I stumble and wince with each step. But I make it and flick the light on.

Blinding. Bright. I shield my eyes and fight the urge to cry.

"Devon. I'm okay, but—" My phone dies. "Dammit."

I reach for the door only to find the knob removed. "Double dammit." Can this night get any worse?

I stash my phone back in my corset top. My eyes adjust to the bright light in this small space, and I take a second to evaluate my own condition. A steel shelf on one wall offers some reflection. The side of my head is covered in dried blood. My own, apparently.

A deep bruise is forming around my right temple, stretching out to my eye. My body feels sore but looks unscathed. Did she drag me? I'm sure more bruises will be making an appearance soon. Worst of all, my gorgeous gown is a wreck. What had Calypso Day said? Not to ruin this dress the first time I wore it? And that's exactly what happened.

Wait. How is this the worst of my problems? I'm locked in a damn storage room and probably suffering from a concussion. A crazy ass, lying woman attacked me tonight. And I don't have a way to get ahold of Devon again.

Sorry, dress. You're the least of my worries.

I look at the door. It looks like she removed the knob from this side, but not from the other. What the hell kind of a plan was this? I peek down into the giant hole where the knob should be, staring at the metal mechanism that's keeping me imprisoned here.

Fortunately, I'm no idiot. *Hear that, Natalia. Screw you and your juvenile attempts at trapping me.* I'm in a storage closet, surrounded by random tools and materials. It takes all of two seconds to find a screwdriver. Not sure what to do with it, but I'm certain I can take things apart until the whole door falls down. I thrust the screwdriver into the door's hole, looking for any parts that seem like they'll move.

There's one. When I put the screwdriver into a small hole in the metal, something jiggles. I twist it and push and pull and beg the thing to do something. I yell at it and ram my entire, aching body into the wood door...

And it gives. I tumble into a hallway. Yes! I am woman, hear me roar. Never mind how much grace that lacked.

But now where am I? This hallway is completely empty, darker than I'd expect, and has very few doors. But my adrenaline is pumping, and I know Devon is looking for me. I pick a direction and walk—limp—as fast as I can. Each door, I pass, I open. More closets, a small office. This has to be an employee-only area.

But a break in one wall renews my hope. I turn down into another hallway, and after trying a few doors (all locked), I find one that's extra familiar.

A stairwell. Apparently, I'm on the second floor. Seriously, how'd Natalia get me here? Did she have help? By the way I feel, I can only assume she dragged me, unconscious, banging me into every wall and step on the way.

I start down the stairs, struggling with each. What time is it? Only hours ago, Devon and I were in here...

I reach the bottom step and stare at the wall Devon had pressed me against earlier. Emotions rush at me faster than Natalia hitting me with a block of solid wood. How had it all gone so wrong? Tears burn my eyes, and it hurts like hell to wipe them away. The gala. Spending the night with Rhys and Christopher and Maddie and Devon. It had been perfect. Devon took Maddie home. We made plans to stay here for the night. It feels like so long ago, but it wasn't. How long was I unconscious?

I take a deep breath trying to regain my focus. Just find Devon. But I can't peel my eyes away from the stairs. My heel digging into that last step holding me steady. The feeling of Devon's mouth on my skin—of the orgasm that took hold of me. He'd felt so good in me—his strong arms holding me up. It had been sexy and thrilling. Hell, we'd almost been caught. Was the intruder Natalia? My stomach turns at the thought. I have to get out of here.

Out through the door, exiting into the main hallway, I walk toward the gala room, forcing down the waves of nausea. My body's so weak, and my ego crushed. I'm embarrassed by how naive I was to have trusted Natalia.

"Olivia!"

I turn toward his voice. There he is. My Devon. I'll be okay now. He rushes to me, cupping my face in his hands. It hurts, but I don't care.

"My god, what did she do to you?"

"I—I don't remember it all. She hit me. With those memorial plaques that were on the tables."

"She hit you with a photo of your brother? That's really fucked up."

Then I can't help myself. I start laughing. It's uncontrollable, but what else do I do in this ridiculous situation? It wasn't that long ago that I was normal, simple Olivia. All the things that made me nervous and cautious in my old life—those were nothing compared to what I'm experiencing now.

"Do I need to take you to the hospital?" Devon asks.

"No. Or...maybe? I don't know. Do you know what the hell is going on? Why did Natalia attack me?"

I lean into Devon letting him support me. He walks me to a cozy lounge area so I can sit down while he explains. The hotel is asleep at this point. I hear someone at the front reception, but otherwise, all is quiet. It's a little creepy after the night I've had.

"Her real name is Natasha," Devon says. "I have a restraining order against her, but clearly that's not keeping her away anymore."

"You know her?"

"Yeah. And I feel bad I couldn't protect you. I had no idea you were working with her. How is it possible I never saw her?"

I think back to the times Devon and Natalia—*Natasha*—were in the same place. The restaurant when we first met up—where she'd changed locations at the last minute. The TV shoot—where she disappeared for most of it. The gala itself tonight—where she stayed in the background. I only saw her when Devon was away from our table. Holy shit, she's been orchestrating this whole thing.

"She's one sneaky bitch."

"You're telling me. Remember when I told you about those phone calls I was getting? The ones I thought were coming from you while we were apart?" He rests his hand on my leg. A tingle rushes through me, and all my conflicted feelings and aches and pains and urges make me want to scream.

Instead I nod in understanding. "I told you it wasn't me. My number wouldn't come up as Unknown." Then another thought occurs to me. "Crap. The first time she came to my apartment, I was talking to Maddie. When I walked back to the living room to talk to Natalia—*Natasha*. I'm just calling her Nat. My head hurts too much to keep it straight. Anyway, when I came back out, she was gone. She'd been in my room. She said she was lost. That's where my phone was. That's how she got your number."

"It sickens me more that she knows where you live."

I shrug. "I'm too dazed to think about that. Where is she now? Creeping around outside my apartment? In another state?"

"Upstairs," Devon answers. "Cuffed to the bed."

Why would she be? An image comes to me. Gross. She was going to *seduce* Devon while I was trapped in a closet?

"What do we do now?"

"For one, I'm calling in my guys and getting ahold of my lawyer. This psycho's getting locked up."

In a matter of minutes, two guys in black suits show up. They're big, beefy, security detail-types. We meet them in the lobby, and I'm sure the sight of me—the blood dried to my face—is enough confirmation that calling them out this late was justified.

We load into the elevator and make our way to the top. I stifle another fit of giggles. This should've been me, hours ago. On my way up to wait for Devon. Tonight should've ended on a high note—the two of us naked in his bed. Instead, I'm a beat-up mess still trying to grasp what's happening. Devon's holding my hand, his free hand clenched into a fist, and two big dudes with guns escort us up to Natalia—*dammit, Nat.* She's going down.

The elevator dings and we pile out.

"We've got this Mr. Stone." One of the guards takes Devon's key card and unlocks the door. Devon and I stand back, staying in the hallway, his arms wrapped securely around me. It's like he really does feel bad about all this, as though it's his fault.

"I'm sorry, Olivia. I shouldn't have left you."

"You couldn't have known." I turn to face him. "None of us knew. And you're here now. It'll be okay."

I focus on him rather than the scene that must be occurring inside the penthouse. When I see that bitch's face...On second thought, I need to prepare for Devon's reaction. He's going to want to kill her. I rest my head on his chest listening to the pounding of his heartbeat.

"Mr. Stone?" one of the guards calls from inside. "The room's clear."

"What does that mean?" I ask. "That lingo for *it's safe to enter*?"

"Guess so." He takes my hand and we walk in together, our heads held high.

"Sir. There's no sign of her. The suite's completely empty."

An empty room, empty bed, and an empty feeling in my stomach.

Where the hell is she?

CHAPTER TWO

One trip to a doctor. One concussion recovery. One sexy Devon insisting I stay with him at the Stone mansion—better security, he says. And here I am, on a Monday evening, basking in the sun on the Stones' private beach. I'm a lucky girl. Not only is Nat long gone, running from her own crazy crimes, but I have Devon Stone—my Lust List Number Three—all to myself.

I adjust the top of my bikini and drink from my frozen daiquiri. The sound of the waves threatens to lure me to sleep. I've never felt more relaxed—

"Hey."

I scream and jump out of my chaise lounge, my heart pounding.

"Whoa. Did I scare you?"

Devon stands next to me, and even though I see with my own eyes that it's just him— that I'm not in any danger—my pulse still races. "No, not scared. You just...just surprised me." I can't get past this skittishness. Everything startles me, like I'm expecting to be attacked again at any moment.

"Right. Like I believe that. Come here." He wraps his arms around me, and I feel myself calming down.

I'm safe. Everything's okay.

Devon's hands press against my back, and the warmth from his fingertips rushes to my skin, sending heat through my body.

"Dinner's waiting inside. You hungry?"

He looks down at me and I steal a kiss. "Definitely hungry, but not for food."

"Yeah?" He leans in close to my ear and the warmth from his breath makes me shiver. "I can take care of that. Again."

Without a word, I turn and lead him toward the steps of the veranda. We walk past the pool, and I step under the outdoor shower to get the beach sand off of me.

Devon's watching, so I make a show of it—make it worthwhile for him. I start the water and step underneath the rainfall-like stream. The water drenches my hair, droplets dripping down my half-naked body. I turn away from Devon knowing damn well he'll be staring at the back of me. The water rinses over my curves, and I run my hands down my hips, looping a finger on each side of my bikini bottoms. I tug just enough to show him some extra skin and then release the elastic and rub my hands back up my sides and through my hair.

One second, I'm alone under the water. The next second, Devon is pressed up behind me, kissing my shoulders, running his own hands down my waist.

I turn to him, holding back my urge to laugh as his button-down shirt and jeans soak up more and more water. This is a sexy moment. I can't let my own giddiness ruin it. Instead, I kiss him, long and hard, pushing my body into his. His hands find their way to my ass, and then he brings one around the front and teases my most sensitive spots with his fingertips. I step up on my tiptoes and moan into his ear. A growl escapes Devon, and he holds me tighter. We need to get inside. Now.

"Mr. Stone," someone interrupts from the back door. "A phone call for you."

Devon gives an exasperated sigh. "We'll continue this soon."

He turns and goes inside, water dripping off his clothes.

I grab a towel and wrap it around myself, trying to ignore the wanting in my body. I go upstairs and change into dry clothes. Back downstairs, I find the dining room table covered in a spread of delicious-looking food. A bright, colorful salad, a tray of fresh fruit, a basket of steaming French bread, roasted potatoes, blackened fish, and a bottle of wine. This world of luxury is like a nonstop vacation. To think, Devon grew up with this.

Sitting down, I pour a glass of wine, stalling as I wait for Devon. I snag a strawberry and nibble on that, wondering who'd be calling him. He seems so busy all the time, yet, he doesn't really have a career. He helps out at the family law office on occasion, but I've yet to see him show any real passion for a job. I want to know what drives him, what he wants to do with his life. He seems to hide that ambitious side of him, but I see it. He's dedicated to his family's business. He's loyal to whatever they need. Maybe he just hasn't found his role in it all. It must have been hard, watching his father give Kaidan everything.

But didn't Devon do it to himself? His family is completely aware of the drug issue.

They probably made the right choice not giving him the keys to the Stone legacy.

I gulp. I'm definitely not delving into this topic over dinner. I can imagine how quickly it can take a turn for the worse.

My phone buzzes in my pocket. Maddie's been checking on me often, so I pull it out grateful that we can chat for a minute before dinner.

A text waits for me, and when I see it, I almost choke on the piece of strawberry in my mouth.

No, this can't be happening.

It's definitely not Maddie.

It's Nat.

It's not just a text message either. A photo's attached. A photo of me and Devon from mere moments ago—under the outside shower, kissing.

And the message that goes with it:

You can't keep me out, bitch.

My breath catches in my throat. My hands shake. This isn't over. She's not gone. And we're not safe here like Devon assured.

I shove my phone back in my pocket and clench the edge of the table with both hands, trying to steady the trembling.

My head is feeling better. The bruises are fading. Fear and anger is finally leaving me more determined to be stronger, rather than crippled with anxiety.

And now this?

Devon walks in, freshly changed into a dry t-shirt and cargo shorts. He looks relaxed and...and happy. I can't ruin what's been happening between us. Things are so good. I can't let Nat drive a wedge between us. I *won't* let her.

"Everything okay?" I ask, not wanting him to ask me the same.

"Yeah. Family drama. You know how it is." He takes a seat and starts filling both our plates with our dinner.

I've only been here a couple days, and I definitely know what he means about *family drama*. The Stones are either coming or going in an urgent rush or they're preparing for court dates, meeting with publicists, fighting on the phone with an array of people. Honestly, I wouldn't want to know all the details. It would leave me stressed out. But it seems like the Stones have enemies, and from what I can tell, I'd never take on a battle against a Stone. I'm lucky to be on their good side.

Halfway through our meal, Kaidan wanders in and collapses in one of the empty chairs, picking up a chunk of fresh bread and chomping into it.

"Help yourself," Devon says with a sarcastic tone.

I haven't seen the two of them together much. Devon says they've been fighting lately, so every time Kaidan comes home, I try to find a way to distract Devon. Have I mentioned how much I hate conflict?

"Need a drink?" Devon asks, this time without the condescending attitude.

"The weekend I had? I need two."

Devon grabs the wine bottle, but Kaidan waves a hand. "Nah. I got this." He gets up and walks to a buffet table lining one wall. He opens a door to reveal a small liquor cabinet. After dropping a couple ice cubes into three lowball glasses, he fills each with a couple shots of amber liquid. He balances the three glasses in a hand, and places one in front of each of us.

"Thank you," I say. I take a gulp letting the heat of scotch settle my nerves. A second gulp, and I don't give a damn about Nat. I got the guy. She'll never have a chance, and Devon won't let her get near me again.

An awkward silence looms between all of us until Devon speaks first. "Have you two formally met?" He points in my direction.

Kaidan stares into his glass. "We've crossed paths."

There's a coldness in both their voices, and my own pulse quickens, expecting a time bomb to go off between these two dysfunctional twins. Any minute now.

"What's going on with that T.R. deal?" Kaidan asks his brother.

I sit back, sipping at my drink.

Devon finishes a bite of his dinner and looks at me. "He's talking about Turbulent Ray. You heard of him?" I shake my head no. "Well, you will. Once I convince him to sign a deal with us."

Us? Is Devon working with Kaidan now?

Devon continues, "He's a hip hop artist. Young, incredibly talented, incredibly egotistical."

Kaidan takes over, "So that's when Devon gets involved. We send him after the tough recruits—the ones who need to be carefully manipulated."

"What? Is that your specialty or something?" I ask Devon. Him doing all this for the label is news to me, but it explains why he travels often.

"Something like that," he says, giving me a wink. "Most people fall for my charming ways."

I playfully kick at him under the table. "I bet they do."

"Speaking of T.R., I'm leaving in the morning to meet him in Atlanta. I'll have the contract signed before I get back. Trust me."

Kaidan doesn't look worried. This really must be a normal thing for them. Call me intrigued. I thought these two wanted to kill each other.

"Wait, you're leaving tomorrow?" Some warning would've been nice.

"It's just for a day. I'll be gone early in the morning and back twenty-four hours later. You can just hang out around here until I'm done. Mark's around if you want to go anywhere, and the staff will take care of the rest."

That doesn't sound so bad. It's just a day in this crazy place. And if Devon's on the other side of the country, Nat won't be able to mess with him—unless she also has a private jet.

"This guy's going to try to suck everything out of you," Kaidan says, lifting his drink. "It's like they don't understand or appreciate how much we invest in them far beyond handing them an advance."

Devon laughs, "They don't know how record labels work."

"You must have stories," I say. "What's it like going after these people?" By now the scotch has turned most my body into a jello-y cloud. Even the text from Nat isn't bothering me. I could kick her ass any day, as long as this liquid courage is involved.

"Devon went to this one band," Kaidan starts. "This rock band who'd been producing all their stuff independently for years. They had a huge fan base, they made music that sounded truly original—none of that ripoff shit we have soliciting us all the time—and we wanted them on our label. We heard they were hard to please—cocky after proving they could succeed without the big industry back-ers. So we sent Devon, and..." Kaidan holds off on the punch line, instead finishing his drink and standing up to get more. "Go ahead, D. Tell her what they got you to do."

Devon rolls his eyes, not nearly as amused as Kaidan. "Turns out, they were huge gam-ers, like role playing video game addicts. They made me join their online guild and bat-tle orcs all night."

Kaidan bursts into laughter behind me.

"You can't be serious," I say.

"Oh, I'm serious. The lead singer played a warlock in the game. He kept yelling at me all night to drop something called the Rain of Fire while he—what was the word he used? While he *aggro-ed* the boss." He shakes his head. "I swear I heard the incessant clicking of keyboard keys in my sleep for days after I got back home."

Now I'm laughing along with Kaidan. I mean, come on. Just picturing all that is priceless.

"You two wouldn't be laughing if it had been you." He plucks a cherry tomato from the salad and launches it at Kaidan's head.

Kaidan calmly dodges it and returns to his seat. "It wasn't that bad."

"Like hell it wasn't. Care to finish the story for me?" Devon goes back to eating, anticipating what Kaidan will say next. Something tells me they share this story more often than Devon would admit.

Kaidan sits up higher in his seat turning toward me. "So Devon makes it through a twelve-hour nerd marathon. And just as the sun is rising, and the promise of a new day embraces him—"

"Cut the poetic shit," Devon says.

Kaidan smirks, "They break it to him they've already signed to Rev Records."

"Ouch," is my only reaction. I try to hide the urge to laugh. It's still so ridiculous.

"I think he secretly enjoyed himself," Kaidan pretends to whisper.

"Right, asshole. That shit is right up my ally. You know? As soon as your girlfriend gets here, I'm coming up with some hilariously awful story about you. Deal?"

"Good luck with that. She's not coming. But that reminds me." Kaidan looks at me again, clearly drunk. "You're not using Devon to get famous or to steal his money or something, correct?"

"Of course I am." I say with a perfectly straight face. Liquor has me feeling confident and goofy, but I quickly realize I shouldn't be joking. Kaidan's not amused. "Sorry, I didn't realize you were being serious. I'm not using Devon. Why would you think that?"

"Seems to be going around..."

Now things are awkward. "Well, I'm not like that." I glance over at Devon, but he's hardly reacting. Is this normal conversation to them?

"Just checking," Kaidan says. But his tone has shifted, like he's off in the distance thinking about something else—or *someone* else. Is he having problems with Hayley?

"Not to pry, but you and Hayley make a great couple. You guys okay?"

Instead of answering, he asks a different question. "How many chances are too many? I mean, how many times can someone mess up or act like an asshole before it's too much, and there's no fixing things?"

Again, I can't tell if he's talking about himself or Hayley or even Devon. It sounds like a familiar situation. Devon catches me glancing over at him and raises his hands up in defense.

"What? Come on. Kaidan's a much bigger asshole than me." He gives a long pause. "Okay, most of the time... Sometimes. But we can't help it. We're twins. We share the asshole gene."

I simply smile at him. He's been sweet lately, but I'm not letting him off the hook that easily. If he's trying to be better, he can keep doing it for a while. It takes time to form a habit, after all, so it also takes time to break one.

"You just have to try," I tell Kaidan, knowing Devon will probably take this to heart too. "Be genuine. If you care, show it. It doesn't have to be that complicated. And if you—or whomever—put in the effort, then it doesn't matter how many chances you give them. Each one will be worth it."

I finish my scotch and move back to my wine. It feels like we're a couple of old friends at this point, so I have the courage to ask the next question. "My turn. You two." I point to each of the guys. "What the hell's up with you guys? I've never seen you get along. All you seem to do is fight and resent each other."

"Us?" Kaidan speaks first. "Nah, we're fine. It's just how we are."

Devon continues the thought, making it more apparent just how close they are. "We have each other's backs, no matter what. But sometimes, we have to kick each other's asses in the meantime."

"Especially with Devon and the drinking and—" Kaidan stops short, throwing a look at Devon. "Never mind."

But I know damn well what he was going to say. The drinking *and the drugs*. I wonder if Kaidan's ever said anything to him about it.

The next morning, the sun streams through the huge windows overlooking the ocean, interrupting my sleep. Devon's missing from the space next to me, and I feel instant disappointment. But in his place is a small, white envelope. My heart leaps at the little surprise. Inside the envelope, I find a folded piece of paper with the sexiest chicken scratch handwriting I've ever laid my eyes on, but at this point, I may be bias.

Didn't want to wake you. I'll see you soon, and I'll miss you every minute I'm gone. — Devon

This man drives me crazy! Everything with him is a whirlwind of ups and downs, and I hope, more than anything, this ride can last forever.

Last night had been so relaxing. In fact, the past couple days have been. But getting to spend time and see Devon and Kaidan act like normal brothers—it was nice. All this time, I thought their relationship needed to be fixed, but apparently, it's just fine.

Watching them made me miss my own normal life though. My little apartment. Maddie. The everyday scramble to find a job. But then there's this place—the Stone mansion—with all its luxury and leisure. I have the choice to stay here—to lounge on the beach and eat gourmet food. How could I pass it up to go back to my simple, sometimes stressful life?

The door bursts open, and I rip at the blanket to pull it up to my chin. *Hello, there's someone in here!* Serena Lynn comes crashing in. I didn't know she and Calvin were back from their weekend trip, but...it's obvious now.

"Can I help you?" I ask.

She ignores me, instead stomping over to the dresser and sifting through the drawers. After an exasperated huff, she moves to a desk, yanking open a drawer, causing it to topple onto the ground. She leans down, pushing things aside.

Standing up, she looks from one side of the room to the other. When her eyes finally land on me, I can see she's crying. Yesterday's eyeliner is smudged to her temples.

"You're not going to get away with this," she says to me angrily.

What the hell is she talking about?

Before I can respond, she moves into the walk-in closet. I listen as things fall to the ground and bang into the walls. She comes back out, holding Devon's duffel bag, the one we'd packed with all my things for my short stay here.

"What are you doing?" I can only handle so much crazy, but she's not just trashing a guest room, she's going through *my* stuff.

"You know damn well what I'm looking for. Where's my necklace?"

"Your necklace? What—"

"Don't play dumb with me." She empties the few things that were in the bag. Unsatisfied, she drops to the floor, looking under the bed. Then she crawls across the Persian rug, searching under all the furniture.

"Um—Serena? I don't have your necklace. I don't even know what you're talking about."

"Oh please. I mention a necklace, and the whole world knows what I'm talking about."

Self-centered much?

She continues, "Huge diamond? Very expensive? You stole it. Ring a bell?"

That big, gaudy thing she wears? If we're being honest, the first time I saw it on her, I thought it was costume jewelry—a big fake. But I quickly felt stupid. It's the Stone family, after all. Of course it would be real. There's no way in hell I'd steal it though.

"I didn't take your necklace. I wouldn't want that thing."

"Of course you would. It's worth more than you make in, what? Ten years, easily. It would pay your rent on whatever trashy apartment you must live in. It would pay for a new car."

Well, when she puts it that way, I can see why stealing it would be worthwhile. I laugh at my own joke.

"You think this is funny?" She gets closer to me. Her excessive use of perfume competes with her obvious morning breath. "I'm going to find it. And when I do, your little butt is going to—"

"What the hell are you doing, Serena?" Kaidan's in the doorway. His fists clenched at his sides.

"Kaidan. You're a lawyer. You can arrest her."

"That's not what lawyers do, genius."

Serena gives him a big pitiful look. "She stole my necklace. You know how much it means to me, and she snatched it with her grubby hands."

Who's she calling grubby? All I can do is look at her in bewilderment. Has she completely lost her mind?

Kaidan looks more angry than he should. This is actually pretty comical.

"I didn't take it," I say. "She doesn't seem to believe me though."

"She didn't take it," Kaidan repeats, glaring at Serena. His face seems to drop as he says each word. "Leave her the hell alone. Get out of here. I'll...I'll look into it for you."

Serena obeys and walks away, defeated.

Kaidan lingers in the doorway a second longer.

"Thank you." He didn't have to stick up for me. "I appreciate it."

"It's nothing." He turns and walks away, closing the door behind him. The pleasantries of last night are clearly over.

Then again, I am sitting in bed, covering my half-naked body with a blanket. Now's not the time for conversation anyway.

I lay back down trying to figure out what the hell that charade was about. Serena just confronted me like I'm a criminal, and why? Because I'm a guest here? Because I'm not a celebrity? Give me a break. A part of me hopes she's lost her ridiculous necklace for good. Maybe it'll teach her a lesson of some sort.

My choice is to stay here, basking in the sun and relaxing or to return home to my *grubby* life.

It's time to get the hell out of here.

CHAPTER THREE

I could have Mark drive me home, but there's
one person eager to come to my rescue—
Maddie. After hanging up with her, it takes
her all of twenty minutes to show up.

"How fast did you drive to get here?" I ask
as I finish grabbing the last of my things. The
room's a mess from Serena's escapade, but
someone else can pick up after her.

Maddie sits on the edge of the bed watching me, a little too excited to be bringing her
best friend back home. "I evaded the cops, so
what does it matter?" She laughs and bounces

lightly on the bed. "This thing is comfortable. A good sex bed."

I throw a clean pair of socks at her, hitting her upside the head. She grabs a throw pillow and retaliates.

"I've missed you," she says.

"I've missed you too. The apartment still in one piece?"

"Of course not. I've been hosting raves every night, your room's been transformed into a meth lab, and I've added five more roommates to the lease to make up for your absence."

Har har. Very funny. "That's some amazing productivity given I've only been gone a couple days."

"Seriously, though. I'm glad you've come to your senses. Who wants to live this insanely rich life anyway?" She pauses a moment. "Oh right, *I* do. Why are you coming back to our crummy apartment anyway?"

"Because there's a lot more to living than money. I want to cook my own meals—maybe even in the microwave. I don't like the feeling of people waiting on me hand and foot."

"Right...Sounds like a nightmare." She rolls her eyes.

"Plus, Calvin and his crazy girlfriend are back, so the Stone mansion vacation is over."

"Ah, a valid reason."

I zip up the duffel bag, certain I haven't forgotten anything *or* accidentally taken something not belonging to me. Who knows the hell Serena would raise if she found out I left with a Stone q-tip.

"All set," I say and lead the way out of the room, down the stairs, and into the foyer.

Before we reach the front door, I hear Kaidan. "Hey, Olivia. Come here a minute...Please."

"Give me a sec," I tell Maddie and follow Kaidan's voice to the study. "What's up? I was just leaving."

"I wanted to say sorry for earlier. Serena's insane. You don't need to leave because of her. And sorry if I was a little weird. There's a lot going on right now."

Kaidan Stone apologizing to me...this *is* weird.

"It's no problem. I need to get back to my life, but I appreciate you all letting me hang out here."

He nods. I assume that's my opening to say goodbye, but then he changes the subject. "He cares about you, you know."

My heart does that flutter thing again.

"I've never seen Devon like this with other girls," Kaidan says, leaning back in his tall leather chair. "Just don't let him get away with his bullshit. You and I both know he needs help. He may not listen to me, but I think he'll listen to you."

"I hope so." I look towards the front door at Maddie and then back at Kaidan. "Thank you for that. And good luck with you and Hayley."

He just shakes his head, and I can't help but feel like I said the wrong thing again. I say bye and hurry back to Maddie.

Goodbye Stone mansion.

We get in her car, and I feel instantly liberated sitting in the passenger seat of a ten-year-old Toyota with non-tinted windows. Back to normal.

We weave our way down the long driveway, passing the carefully pruned hedges and tall green trees. But as we near the gate, it looks like leaving won't be so easy.

"What's going on?" Maddie asks.

The iron gates are closed, and Roger, the gate guard, is talking to one of the Stone's security detail. The guy's dressed in a black suit, sunglasses, and one of his hands holds firmly to the cuffed wrists of a woman they have in custody.

The woman is clearly distraught, yelling at the men, and it takes me no time at all to recognize her.

Her pixie cut dark hair. A cropped black tank top. Smokey eyeshadow.

It's Lex.

"Holy shit. It's Devon's sister."

"Then why is she being arrested?" Maddie stops in front of the closed gate.

"Good question." I reach over and tap the horn to get Roger's attention. He looks over but holds up an index finger, telling me to wait.

I get out of the car and get as close as I can.

"Roger, what's wrong?"

"Olivia?" Lex says, looking instantly relieved to see someone she knows. But this is the same girl who wouldn't give us the time of day in Oregon. I'm not sure what she's hoping I'll do here.

Roger walks over. "Mr. Stone informed me there's a woman following you all. We have reason to believe she—"

"And I already told you I'm fucking family, you asshole." Lex yanks against her restraints again. This time, the security guy opens the backseat of his SUV and pushes her inside.

Roger sighs. "Once she's away from the area, I'll open the gate for you two."

"She's telling the truth," I say. By now Maddie's at my side, intrigued by the sudden drama.

"According to her, she's the sister of—"

"Half-sister. They share the same mother. Devon and I just found out. I think he told Kaidan, too. And I'm sure Calvin knows Melody Hastings had another kid."

"Damn. I haven't heard that name in years," Roger says. "But I still can't let her in."

"But you can't arrest her either. Just let me talk to her." Not sure what I'll say, but she must be here for a reason.

Roger hesitates but then signals to the other guy to let Lex out. He brings her over to the gate.

"What are you doing here?" I ask. She looks like a wreck, like she hasn't showered in a week.

"It's all gone, Olivia." She starts to sob. "All my money. My apartment. I got evicted. I'm broke."

"So you came down here because?"

"Because it's all fucking your fault." She kicks the gate, and the guard yanks her away from it putting more space between us.

"How is it our fault?"

"Your people found out about me. They contacted the lawyer in charge of the will. They'd assumed mom was alive all this time accepting her payout, but when they found out she died, the money stopped."

Should I feel bad about this? I mean, we didn't intentionally do anything to hurt her. She could just as easily get a job to support herself—but even I know that's sometimes easier said than done.

"I'm sorry, I guess. But what do you want from us?"

"You have it all. A cozy, stupid mansion. All the money in the world. Power to go with it."

Does she know who she's talking to? "Lex, you have no idea—"

"Oh, fuck off, Princess," she yells. "What the hell do I do? I get kicked out. I have nothing left. Nothing. I hitched a ride down here just to kick your ass."

"And you know I can tell these guys right here to take you in, right? What the hell is wrong with you?"

Roger speaks up. "We suspect she's under the influence of an illegal substance. Likely, cocaine."

Well, great. Just what I want to deal with—*two* Stones dealing with drug issues.

"Just take her down to the station," Roger says. "We'll deal with her—"

"No," I interrupt. "If she can calm down, I'll find a way to help her."

"You sure?" Maddie asks, resting her hand on my shoulder. "You don't owe her anything."

"I don't, but...I don't know. Lex, aside from kicking everybody's asses, what do you need?"

She's back to crying. "I don't know what to do, Olivia. I'm sorry. I'm fine. I'll be cool. I'm just so...lost right now. My mom. My home."

I'm not sure if she's being genuine or if she's faking her own pity party, but what option do I have? I can't just ditch her.

I take a deep breath hoping I don't regret my words as quickly as I say them. "She can come with us. I'll get ahold of Devon." I turn to Lex. "But these guys," I point to both guards, "will be waiting for my call. You pull any crap with me, and that's it. No more help."

She nods in agreement, and Roger opens the gate. Maddie gets in her car and pulls forward while I walk through and approach Lex. The moment the handcuffs are removed, she throws her arms around me in a shaky hug. "Thank you, Olivia. You're the only friend I have."

Yeah, she's definitely high.

CHAPTER FOUR

Maddie drives while I try to reach Devon, and Lex stretches across the backseat, in a daze.

"Where's your stuff, Lex?" I ask. Devon's phone keeps going to voicemail. I hang up and turn towards the backseat.

"In my pocket," she mutters. Then she reaches into her shorts pocket and pulls out a little bag of white powder. She clutches it in her fist like it's her lucky gold coin.

I shake my head. Why the hell did I get deeper into this mess? First Devon, now Lex. What am I, the intervention queen?

"That's not what I meant. Your clothes, your belongings. Where are they?"

"I was locked out of my apartment. It's all back there. When I went home last night, I tried to break the door, but then the stupid whore of an apartment manager called the cops, and I had to run. I stopped a trucker on his way down the highway, and he said he could get me down here in exchange for..." She stops to watch out the window again, this time looking off at the coast.

Oh god, please don't tell me she prostituted herself out just to come to L.A.

Maddie glances over at me with a worried look on her face. What are we going to do with her?

Finally, Lex speaks again. "He said he could get me down here in exchange for a line of coke."

For a second I feel relieved, but that just means a doped-up trucker drove her here. They could've been killed. At least a blowjob would've been less...dangerous to all of society? I have no idea how to take this. I'm in way over my head.

"Lex, don't you think that was dangerous?"

She starts laughing—cackling, in fact. "Oh, Livi, are you some sort of goody goody or something? That's fucking precious."

And now we've moved on to insults.

"Maddie, we could just drop her off on the side of the road. She seems to like the beach. She can probably find a bridge to sleep under."

Maddie starts to slow the car to emphasize my threat.

"Okay, okay." Lex sits up in the backseat and reaches forward embracing me from behind. "I'm sorry, again. You're just, really nice. It's weird."

"Maybe you've been hanging around the wrong people."

"My mom always said that too."

Before I can address this strange confession, my phone starts ringing. There's Devon.

"Olivia, what's wrong?"

"Nothing's wrong. What makes you think that?"

"Because you've called me six times in the last ten minutes."

Oh right. I guess, with everything that's happened recently, that would look bad. "Sorry. Nothing's wrong. Well, not exactly. I'm with Maddie. We were leaving the mansion, and...and we ran into Lex."

"This is a practical joke right? Not funny."

"Nope, not funny at all. She's currently in the backseat."

I hold the phone toward Lex, who shouts into the receiver, "Hi, big brother!"

I put the phone back to my ear. "See?"

"What the hell is she doing? In Oregon, she was a bitch, telling me off. Why would you have her in the car with you?"

"Because she needs help, and we're the type of people who help others."

"Correction," Devon says. "*You're* the type who helps. I couldn't give a damn what she needs after the way she acted. Tell her to leave town. We don't want her around."

"Devon, that's not going to happen. We need to—"

"We don't *need* to do anything." His voice gets louder before he catches himself. "We owe her nothing. Now, I have a meeting. I'll talk to you later."

He hangs up before I can say anything else.

"So? How's the big D?" Lex asks from the backseat, giggling to herself after catching on to her unintended dirty joke.

At the gate, Maddie said we owed Lex nothing. Now Devon's saying it too. Am I the only one who feels family helps out family no matter how awful they may have been?

I store my phone back in my purse and breathe out a frustrated sigh. "Devon's fine. He'll be back tomorrow, and we'll talk to him. Until then, you can stay with me and Maddie." Looking over to Maddie, I give her my best apologetic expression. "That's okay with you, right?"

My best friend catches on to my pleading tone and grips my hand as reassurance. Then she calls to the backseat in a cheerful voice, "Yep! It'll be great."

We get to the apartment, and I feel a weight lift from my shoulders. Even with Lex in tow and a stalker somewhere out there, I feel much better now. I'm home.

Maddie unlocks the door, and I'm overwhelmed by the sight of our living room.

Balloons. Streamers. Flowers. A big box of cupcakes.

I pull Maddie into a hug. "You did all this for me?"

"You should've never been left alone at the gala. I acted like a child and got trashed. Devon, Mr. Cavalier, got me back here safely, and while he was here, that awful bitch was hurting you."

"It's done with. And it wasn't your fault. Okay?" I look around at our apartment. She's even spent time cleaning it. The usual dust bunnies hiding under the edges of the couches are missing. "You didn't have to go through all this trouble."

"I didn't have much else to do." She shrugs, then gets a grossed out look on her face. "What's that smell? The trash is empty. I even had candles burning."

We turn to find Lex leaning against the wall smoking a cigarette.

Maddie looks at me, annoyed. "It smells like my bar."

I glare at Lex. "Outside. Be considerate."

"Whatever." She mopes out of the apartment.

I shake my head. "I don't know what I'm doing."

"Yeah, neither do I."

I grin at her. *Thanks, best friend.* "I just can't *not* help her. But she's more a mess than..."

"Than Devon?"

"Yes. And he wants nothing to do with her. So I'm working double duty. I need to fix their relationship *and* get her clean."

Maddie grips both of my shoulders and looks at me seriously. "You do know you don't *have* to do anything, right? I love you for how much you want to help, but these aren't your battles, and they're adults."

I know she's right, but it still feels like the thing I need to do. There's no talking me out of this one.

"I'm going to get unpacked. Thank you, so much, for everything. I don't know what I'd do without you."

We have another cheesy, sappy moment before I disappear to my room. I laugh when I see she's even tidied my room. The bed's made, the curtains are pushed open, letting sunlight cascade through, and an enormous bouquet of white lilies and roses waits on my dresser.

This is sweet, but Maddie shouldn't feel so guilty. None of us expected Nat to be a complete lunatic. I empty the duffel bag, making a mental note to get my own if I'm going to keep spending nights away from my apartment. I replace all my things in their respective homes—wouldn't want to mess up Maddie's work—and then return to the gorgeous flowers on my dresser. A little envelope is tucked inside the middle, and I pluck it out, anticipating another heartfelt apology from Maddie.

Another punch in the gut.

These aren't from Maddie.

Better luck next time. ~N.V.

Nat Vorhees. I'm only just now noticing her initials sound like "envy". Did she make that up too? Who would ever envy her? Or maybe I'm just being paranoid.

I grab my phone and storm out of the room. Maddie's in the kitchen.

"Who brought those flowers?" I demand.

She spins around. "Whoa. What's wrong?"

"The bouquet on my dresser. Who brought it here?"

She thinks for a second. "I assume the florist delivery people." She rolls her eyes and smiles. "They were waiting at the door when I got home yesterday. Why?"

"They were sent by Nat." I sit down and pull up yesterday's text message on my phone.

"What a creep," Maddie says, joining me.

Lex returns from outside, wanders through the living room, and disappears into the bathroom. Normal people have errands to run, bills to pay, and a house to clean. I have drug addicts to intervene, relationships to repair, and a stalker to evade.

I rub the growing ache in my head and push the phone to Maddie. "It gets worse." I give her a second to put it all together. "That photo was taken minutes before she sent it. She's following me. I don't think she's finished."

Maddie shakes her head in disgust. "Then we stop her before she can hurt you again."

She takes my phone and walks into the living room. "Is this her personal phone number?" Then I hear her mumble quieter, pressing the phone to her ear. "For a longtime stalker, she sort of sucks at it."

"I don't know what phone that is. It's the same number she used while we were planning the gala. Maybe it's a work phone or..."

"You listen very carefully," Maddie says into the phone, her voice as serious and threatening as sweet Maddie can be. "You will not go near Olivia again. Or Devon for that matter. You have no idea who you're messing with, and if you think you can lay a finger on my best friend again, you have another thing coming to you ... You will regret every stupid move you've made, and jail time won't be an issue because I'll make sure your crazy ass is stuck in a hospital for a very...long...time. Do I make myself clear? No more of these games ... Got it? ... Good."

She hangs up and I exhale the breath I'd been holding. "What did you just do? What did she say? Did she take you seriously?"

Maddie hands my phone back. "I don't know. I got her voicemail."

"You're insane. Maybe not Nat-insane. But what if you just added fuel to the fire?" I point to my phone. "You saw that photo. She could be outside our door right now."

The doorbell rings, and we both jump. We sit here, frozen, staring at each other, when Lex comes out of the bathroom and looks at us.

"What's wrong with you two?" She walks to the door and opens it wide. No crazy stalkers rush in, so that's a relief. "I'll be back later."

Lex lets the door shut behind her.

"Who does she know in L.A.?" Maddie asks.

I raise both hands in an "I have no clue" gesture. Maybe I should've stayed at the mansion. At this point, Serena Lynn doesn't even show up as a speck on my stress radar.

CHAPTER FIVE

I survived Day One being back in my supposedly simple life. Nat didn't try sneaking through my window while I slept, and her flowers are out in the dumpster—thanks to Maddie. Devon's back from Atlanta, and we're meeting up for lunch. I completely dropped the Lex subject, and he seems to be in a great mood. That'll probably change when he sees Lex with me, but these two are talking today—face-to-face—whether he wants it or not.

My phone alarm goes off. Yeah, I know. I'm supposed to be past this, but I already said old habits die hard, and something about that familiar ringing makes me feel in control of all my current problems. This alarm is to remind me to get Lex up and ready...and to make sure she doesn't get high between now and lunch. I want her sober when they talk.

I won't mention the alarm set for when it's time to leave, especially since even I know I don't need an alarm to tell me to go see Devon. In fact, it looks pitiful having a reminder to have lunch with my boyfriend, doesn't it? On second thought, yeah, it's definitely unnecessary. *Get a grip, Olivia.*

I disable the extra alarms—the one for lunch, the ones set for later and tomorrow. No more of that. I can take care of myself. It's time to step up. I can't really take control of things if I don't have control over my own head. So it starts now. I go a step further and delete all the alarms—every one of them telling me what to do and when to do it. Alarms from years ago telling me to get ready for classes or make dinner. Ones from weeks ago telling me to leave for my interview with Mr. Keenly—the interview that changed my entire life.

The alarms don't own me. My problems don't own me. Nat doesn't own me.

I hold my head up higher. *Let's do some good today, O.*

Outside of my room, the rest of the apartment is quiet. Maddie's room is empty. No one's in the bathroom. And Lex isn't here.

How the hell am I supposed to get her ready to go when she's not even here? Did she come home last night?

No problem. Just a minor glitch. There's still time, so I'll wait for her. She'll turn up—hopefully before we need to leave.

An hour later, I'm trying not to glance at the clock too frequently. I'm scrubbing dishes from breakfast and relaxing my breathing. Then I hear the door open, and I'm tempted to turn around and chastise Lex like a child coming home after curfew. But I remember what Maddie said. She's an adult. I have to respect that.

"Want coffee?" I ask, not looking at her.

She lets out a moan and I hear her plop down on the couch. "No...I'm good," she says in a drawn out sing-song voice.

Now I look over and find her in her own little trance, gazing up at the ceiling fan. Dammit, she's high already?

I bite my tongue, not wanting her to go into an aggressive rage like yesterday at the gate. "We have plans today. Lunch. Can you...um...try to sober up before then?"

She lets her head roll in my direction and smiles. "You need a hit. Or you need to get laid. You got a boyfriend?"

Is she serious?

"I'm with Devon. Remember?"

Lex starts laughing. "Right, right. My big bro. I love that guy."

Give me a break. She's too far gone to ne-
gotiate with now. I go in my room, find her a
change of clothes, and return, tossing the
outfit on the cushion next to her.

"Go take a shower. Clean up." *In more
ways than one.* "We're leaving when you're
done."

Lex seems a little more human when she
emerges a while later. Refreshed and alert,
she's actually very beautiful. Her pixie cut is
smoothed down, looking chic, instead of being
the wild mess she usually sports. Her eyes are
less puffy after the shower, and in the jeans
and button down blouse I loaned her, she
looks mature, approachable.

My hope is restored. "How do you feel?" I
ask, standing up and grabbing my purse. I
toss my phone in and grab my keys.

I get a groan from her, but she saunters
over to the couch and steps into her shoes. At
least she's not resisting my plans—not that

she knows what we're doing anymore than Devon knows.

In the car, I get on the highway, heading toward Colin's Diner. I won't lie. I'm nervous, but this is exciting. I'm determined to play mediator for Lex and Devon.

"So...where were you last night?" I try to sound casual, not nagging.

"Long story or short?"

"We have time." I might as well hear all the details. Maybe it'll help me figure out what to do with her.

Lex takes a deep breath. "So while you were gossiping with your girlfriend, I grabbed her phone on my way to the bathroom. I did a couple quick searches and found a dude who could hook me up. My stash was low and if I'm going to be here a while, I need a go-to guy—or girl. I'm not sexist or anything. Anyway, Joe picked me up, and we hit it off. He had a little party at his place, so he introduced me to the local crowd, and I ended up staying the night. That's all."

That's all. "So this Joe guy's a drug dealer. You had him come to my place to pick you up, and you stayed out all night with him—a total stranger?"

"You know? I was going to apologize for yesterday and calling you a goody-goody and everything, but..."

I glare at her. "Should I remind you I can have you re-arrested any moment?"

"Uh huh. Forget it. I'll keep my life to myself so as not to offend you and your values."

"It's not like that, Lex." Count to ten. I want to yell at her that she doesn't know anything about me, but it won't do me any good. "I just don't fully...understand...why you need it." Or why Devon needs it.

Change the subject. I'm in a positive mood, no room for a bunch of negativity. Try to relax. It'll be fine. We're going to meet up with Devon. I'm going to get these two to bond—hopefully not over their addictions.

And here are the bad thoughts again. Okay, new topic.

We get to a red light and stop. I focus on my car.

This thing probably needs a tune up. The tires are low on air. The brakes are a little squishy.

"You mad now?" Lex asks, looking amused.

"No. I'm just...driving."

I step on the gas, now hurrying to get to Devon. But the damn traffic and red lights are keeping me trapped with Lex and my own thoughts.

"Dude," Lex starts. "You really need to chill. You aren't better than me."

"I never said I was."

"And I'm not some sort of loser just 'cause I do stuff you don't like. So you should just stop—"

"I can't."

Oh shit. Something's wrong.

"Can't what? Can't stop judging me? Can't stop acting like—"

"No! I can't stop the car!" The brakes were squishy a minute ago. But now they're...unresponsive. Fuck, fuck, fuck. "I don't know what to do. The brakes aren't working."

The light ahead of us is red. I clench the steering wheel and start hyperventilating.

"You're going to hit that car!" Lex shouts. She grabs the emergency brake and yanks it up.

The car starts to skid, tires squealing against the L.A. street. But we aren't going to stop fast enough. Either we hit the car ahead of us or...

I turn the wheel and steer us into a ditch. The car comes to a stop with a jolt. I throw it in park, and drop my head into my hands, struggling to steady my breathing.

"What the hell just happened?" Lex asks.

"I—I...I don't know. One second, it was okay. The next, they just stopped working."

We get out of the car and walk around to the front as though I can diagnose the problem. The bumper's a little scratched up from the rough stop. A newer car with a warranty would make this much easier. I pull out my phone to call a tow truck and a taxi. Devon's waiting and...

A car pulls up behind us and parks. Both doors open, and I groan when I see who's found us. The cameras start going off almost immediately as the two paparazzi climb out.

"Are they serious?" Lex smirks and I'm startled by the resemblance to Devon.

Laughter escapes me. "Yeah. They show up at the worst times." Adrenaline pumps through me, and the last thing I want to do is deal with the media. They rush toward us, talking over each other.

"Ms. Margot, can you tell us what happened here?"

"Did anyone get hurt, Ms. Margot."

"Is Devon Stone in the car?"

"Were you driving drunk?"

Ignoring them both, I let them snap whatever idiotic photos they want. I find a tow truck guy who can come pick it up and drop it off at a mechanic. I tell him I'll pay him extra if he can handle all this without me present. All I have to do is say my name and that I'm trying to get rid of the paparazzi before he shows up, and the guy's more than happy to take care of my car without me.

Next up, a taxi, so we can get to the diner. Just as I get an answer, one of the paps get in my face.

"You can tell me. Are you on something? Intoxicated? High?"

I recognize this jerk. He's the one I laughed at last time I saw him because he looks like a damn pirate—hoop earring, weird vest. The resemblance must be intentional.

Not that I have the upper body strength to have any effect, but I shove the guy away from me. I think he's trying to smell my breath. What a creep.

I turn away to talk to the taxi service, and Lex squeezes past me, getting in pirate guy's face. I watch her, worried about whether or not she'll make things worse.

"You got a problem, you talk to me." She's fearless, inches away from the creeper's face. "What do you want?"

A taxi will be here in a couple minutes. Now we just need to get away from these vultures.

"I'm just doing my job, babe. If Olivia Margot's wrecking her car in the middle of the day, that's news. And that news can pay me big bucks."

"Hate to break it to you, asshole, but I was the one driving."

"And you are?" He lets his camera hang from his neck as he pulls out a cell phone, turning on a voice recorder and holding it toward Lex to catch her next words.

"Special Agent Iris Copenhagen. I'm on a secret mission with the Queen of Spiked Stilettos here. We're on our way to the Grand Canyon to—"

"You're screwing with me, aren't you?" the dumb pirate says.

I stifle my own laughter.

"No," Lex keeps a perfectly straight face. "I speak nothing but the truth." She moves fast, grabbing pirate pap's phone and chucking it out into the street where it meets its fate with a passing semi truck.

We all hear the crunch of metal and glass as the phone is pulverized against the pavement.

"Oops," Lex says and turns to me. "We ready to go?"

We start walking a few feet down the road while I keep an eye out for our taxi. Behind us, a pissed off pirate yells at Lex, but she doesn't even blink.

A yellow car comes to a stop next to us, and we hop in.

"Colin's Diner, and quickly. The paparazzi are following us."

The taxi driver tells us it's no problem and hits the gas. I'm not sure it's a good idea to leave my broken car with a couple disgruntled paps, but what's the worst that can happen?

"Thank you," I tell Lex. "For stepping up back there. You didn't have to tell them you were driving."

"I never wanted to live down here. Hell, I never wanted to visit down here. But I always thought it'd be fun to tell off the paparazzi. I figured I'd never have the chance."

She has this satisfied look on her face, as though we've just crossed something off her bucket list.

"Well, I'm glad I could make your dreams come true."

CHAPTER SIX

We get to the diner only a few minutes late, thanks to the fact we'd left unreasonably early from the apartment. Devon's waiting on the upstairs terrace. First he spots me, and I get that sexy grin that implies he's relieved to see me, but then his eyes meet Lex's, and his expression vanishes.

"This'll be fun," Lex says under her breath.

"Just wait at the table. Let me talk to him real quick."

I walk to Devon, take his arm, and without saying a word, lead him inside to a quiet hallway.

"What the hell, Olivia?"

"I know. Don't be mad."

He glares down at me, eyebrows raised.

"For starters," I say, leaning up and kissing him. "Welcome back."

He softens a little at that, relaxing his shoulders.

"Now hear me out." I take a breath, ready to defend all of my good intentions. "She needs help. We're going to help her."

Maybe I catch him off guard by my assertiveness, or maybe he just missed me while he was gone, but he smiles. "And why are we helping the woman who slammed a door in our face?"

"Because we won't stoop to that level. Plus, I think...when you talk to her, you'll find she's a lot like you."

"Is that good or bad?" he asks.

"I'll let you be the judge of that."

He steps closer to me, and I'm overtaken by his scent. I close my eyes and soak him in. It's unbelievable how I feel about him.

"One more question," he says quietly in that low, sexy voice.

Want to go back to my place? Want to stay with me forever? Want to elope yesterday?

I'd say yes to all of them right this instant. "Hmm?"

"When were you going to explain this?" Devon holds up his phone to show me the *ScandalLust* article announcing my car accident. A photo shows me on the phone and Lex yelling at the pirate guy. And the article proves to be the icing on the cake.

"Girls Gone Dirty: Devon Stone's Girlfriend, Caught In a Lesbian Love Triangle After Crashing Into Ditch—What Were They Doing in the Front Seat to Cause the Accident? You'll Never Believe It."

"Wow...They work fast." I want to make more jokes, but he's still waiting for an actual answer though. "Sorry. My focus is on this lunch. My car's old. It gave up on me. There's nothing more to it, but those guys were trying to build more drama, obviously."

Devon looks at me for a long second. "You're okay though?"

"Yes. And Lex helped, so you *really* owe it to her to listen. Now let's go."

We go back to Lex, and I'm relieved how easy it was to get Devon to agree to this. I flash Lex an encouraging smile, and we all order our drinks and food. Let this lunch begin.

"So," I start, hoping to help break the ice. "Lex has hit some hard times, and Maddie and I are letting her stay with us. It works out great."

Devon eyes me suspiciously and turns to Lex. "So you couldn't give us the time of day in Oregon, but you have no problem using my girlfriend for your own needs?"

I kick Devon under the table. He's got to stay cool.

"I'm sorry about the way I acted when you guys came up," Lex says. She speaks calmly, and I'm glad to see the effects of her morning high have worn off. "It all caught me off guard, but that's no excuse."

"Fine." Devon grabs his glass of wine as quickly as our server sets it down. He takes a large swallow and pushes his hair back from his face. "So what do you want now?"

"I don't know. I haven't been around family in so long I—"

"I'm family now?" Devon smirks and shakes his head. "Actually, that brings up an important point. I was talking to Kaidan about you."

That's news to me. When did he talk to Kaidan? How did Kaidan react?

Devon continues, "Our family has seen its share of scams. People try to trick us out of our money, our business secrets, our personal freedom. So Olivia and I take a trip to Oregon to find my mother. We find you instead, someone who's been living off money that wasn't hers. Why should I even believe you when you say you're my sister—oh, I'm sorry. *Half-sister.*"

The condescension in his voice couldn't be any thicker. He has a point though. Unfortunately, unless Lex is a great actress, the resemblance between these two is enough of an answer alone.

"You're serious? Why would I lie about that?" She looks genuinely confused by the accusation. It's the same way I reacted to Kaidan asking me if I was using Devon.

"Why? The same reason others do. They want money, fame, power. I don't know. Greedy, selfish people do crazy things."

Lex leans forward visibly pissed off. "If I were greedy *or* selfish, don't you think I would've shown up long ago? You're the one who came and found me. It's not like I plotted some devious scheme to convince you."

"That's the thing. I *need* you to convince me. Now, before this conversation can go any further."

Lex lets out a frustrated sigh and reaches into her back pocket, pulling out her wallet. She opens it and delicately brings out an old, creased photo. I can tell it's been living in that wallet for years.

She lays it down in front of Devon, and I lean over to get a closer look. A young woman sits in a rocking chair with a preschool-aged girl on her lap. Both are beaming with great big smiles.

"Am I to believe this is you and mom?" Devon asks. He tries to keep the same skepticism in his tone, but I see pain flash across his eyes.

"It is," Lex says. Then she pulls out a second photo, placing it next to the first. This one's not tattered and worn. It has the same woman in it—this time holding two newborn babies swaddled in hospital blankets. "This one should look more familiar."

Devon doesn't say a word. Does he still doubt her? Who'd fake these photos? And how would she, anyway—by searching through yard sales until she found a woman who looked like her mom who just happened to be holding twins?

I watch Devon, waiting for him to speak. Instead, he pulls out his own wallet. I hear him let out a frustrated breath—or maybe it's sadness. He lays a picture on top of the others. This photo is bent on one side from getting caught in the fold of the wallet, but it's unmistakable. It's the same exact photo Lex brought.

"You've been carrying that all this time?" I ask him. He didn't even know his mother's name until recently, yet he's had this photo?

"I found it back when I was searching for my father's will. Remember, when I was trying to find out if I'd been written out of it? I wasn't sure this was even me and Kai, but...I was just in denial." He replaces the photo, putting his wallet away.

I turn to Lex, "Do you know what happened—why she left?"

"She was my mom, and I loved her and all, but she was fucked up. I guess she was even worse before I was born." Lex looks at Devon. "She said she was terrified after she gave birth to twins. She couldn't get sober and was a mess and couldn't handle being the mom of one, let alone two babies. Your dad gave her an out—but it came with a sacrifice. He provided her with the means to live comfortably. Granted, she spent a lot of it on drugs, but she was taken care of. And in return, her babies would have a life she could never give them. Then she had me a few years later."

Our table is silent as we let the truth settle in. It's a heartbreaking reality, but it sounds like Melody Hastings made the best decision at the time.

One question still lingers, and I find the courage to ask it. "When did she pass away? What happened?"

Lex collects her photos and carefully puts them back in her wallet. For a second I think she's going to ignore my questions. But she clears her throat and tells us. "She never could get clean. When I was sixteen, she got sick. Sharing needles and whatnot. She stopped coming home, relying solely on her dealer to care for her. He took her money and kept her doped up until she died of an overdose. I think the fucker did it on purpose but..."

How horrible. "You stayed at the apartment?"

"Yeah. I got emancipated. We couldn't find my father, and with no one else around to take care of me, I took care of myself."

I'm not sure that's how I'd word it. Judging by her behavior—getting high, leaving with strangers, being homeless—she seems more like she's following in her—*their*— mother's footsteps.

We finish lunch in contemplative silence. Under the table, Devon takes my hand, caressing each of my fingers with his thumb. I squeeze his hand in a supportive gesture.

Then he looks to Lex. "How can I help you get back on your feet?"

She can't hide the smile and relief that crosses her face. "Right now, I just need a place to stay. And...it'd be nice to get to know my brothers."

I couldn't be happier that these two are getting a chance to build a relationship. I'm so proud of Devon for cooperating, hearing her out. The truth is painful, but so's not having any support, any family. Lex needs him, and I think he needs her. He was holding onto the photo of his mom. He wanted these answers. Now he can get to know his mother through his sister.

"How about we go out tonight?" I pipe in. "We can go to LUSH or something. Lighten the mood and just have some fun."

Devon looks at me like I'm crazy. Lex's eyes brighten.

"Sounds good to me," she says.

We both stare down Devon waiting for his response. "Fine, we'll go out."

I find a couple Calypso Day dresses for us to wear, and Lex and I get all dressed up in my room.

"Thank you," she says, "for earlier, at lunch. I'm not sure he would've talked to me if it weren't for you."

"Yeah, I'm pretty certain he wouldn't have. Kaidan might have been a better one to approach first." I think. I don't know. He seems nice, but that could be the facade he uses to hide his own hardened interior.

"He'll be the next one I talk to...eventually. So what's this LUSH place? A bar?"

I smudge some black eyeliner around my eyes and put on a flattering shade of red lip stain. "It's *the* celebrity spot. It's an exclusive night club that has ridiculous lines down the block."

Lex's shoulders drop. "Hollywood crap? Ugh."

"I had the same thought at first, but it can be fun."

"I'll take your word for it."

I grab a red clutch to match my crimson dress and reach for my phone to toss it inside. Before I do, I notice a voicemail waiting from an unknown number. My pulse quickens at the thought of Nat trying to mess with me again. Should I bother listening?

I let curiosity get the best of me.

Ms. Margot. This is Ron from Auto Care. I had a look at your car, and it seems the damage came from a punctured brake line. It causes the problem to worsen each time you stop until the brakes give out completely. Seems like that's what happened here, so uh—I suggest filing a report with the cops 'cause it looks like you upset the wrong person. This was no accident. Now, if you can give me a call tomorrow...

I hang up before hearing the rest. It wasn't an accident. And it wasn't simply "someone" who punctured the brake line. Obviously, it was Nat. She could've killed us. What the hell is wrong with her?

"You alright?" Lex asks. "Looks like you saw a ghost."

I put my phone away and pretend to check my makeup one last time. "I'm fine." She doesn't need to know about my problems, but I do have to tell Devon. The text message was unwelcome. The flowers were creepy. But this...this is taking it too far. I can enjoy myself tonight. We're safe, and I'll be with Devon. Tomorrow morning though, Devon and I will have to figure out what to do about our psycho stalker.

CHAPTER SEVEN

Mark pulls up in a limo, and Devon—dressed sexy in a black button-down and dark denim jeans—holds the door for us, acting like a gentleman.

"You've got to be kidding?" Lex mutters, looking around the interior of the limo.

Devon opens the mini fridge and pulls out a bottle of whiskey, pouring us each a couple shots into lowball glasses. Before I lift mine to my lips, Devon throws his back, gulping it down quickly and pours another one.

I sip at mine. This stuff burns. What's up with him though? "Everything okay?"

He drops his hand onto my leg, rubbing my thigh. His touch sends shockwaves through me.

"I'm fine," he says, sounding an awful lot like me after listening to my voicemail. "Just have a headache."

I let it go and lean my head against his shoulder. I want us to have a good time tonight and show Lex how she can be happy without the need to hang out with skeezy people.

Mark pulls up to the front of LUSH and walks around to open the door for us. A dozen cell phone cameras flash as we step out. Waiting in line to get in this place must have its own excitement when you see celebrities pull up right in front of you.

Lex keeps her head down, but apparently I've gotten used to this. I send a quick wave to the waiting crowd, and Devon wraps his arm around me, leading us in.

"Couldn't just keep it low-key, could you?" Lex says, irritated by the sudden onslaught of attention.

"Like I said," I tell her, putting my arm around her shoulders, "you get used to it. I swear. I hated it at first, but...it grows on you."

Lex shakes her head, not believing me. "Whatever. I'm going to need another drink if you expect me to hang out with first class snobs all night."

I don't bother arguing. For all of us who came into this bizarre, luxurious life as former outsiders, we carry a number of preconceived ideas. So far, most of my own have been proven wrong. The few celebrities I've talked to—and the one I've been sleeping with—have seemed like nothing more than normal people living extraordinary lives. I used to daydream of being a little starlet, having everything handed to me, but honestly, I wouldn't trade lives with them anyway. We all have our demons, and they aren't excluded.

Devon takes my hand and pulls me toward the back VIP rooms. We pass through a velvet curtain and find a quieter space—dark, more private. A couple couches are filled with people talking and laughing and drinking. I consider the fact no one's doing lines of coke in the middle of the room and decide this is a massive step up from the club Devon brought me to in San Francisco.

"What about Lex?" I say, looking back. Did she see us come in here? I don't want her to think we ditched her.

"What about her? She's a big girl. She can find us if she wants to, but I'll put money on it. The first movie star she recognizes, and she'll be like any other fan girl coming to this city for the first time."

He falls back onto a couch rubbing one hand over his forehead.

"Still not feeling great?" I ask, sitting next to him.

"You could say that." He pulls me closer to him and kisses the top of my head. "You look sexy, by the way."

I feel my cheeks warm. "Thank you."

He traces his fingers down my bare arm, and I shiver. I turn his way and kiss him. The warmth of his mouth, the taste of him, relaxes me and makes me wish this room were even more private.

I pull away and take his hand in my own. Softly, I trail my index finger from his fingertips to his palm. I can't help but notice a tremor in his hand. He's shaking. Is he sick?

"You want to leave? We shouldn't have gone out if you're coming down with something."

He smirks and shakes his head. "I'm not sick, Olivia. I'm just...dealing with stuff."

What does he mean by that?

"Let me get you a drink, okay?" I say. Clearly, he needs to relax. Something's bothering him.

He nods and I go to the VIP bar. A quick glance to the other end of it, and I recognize an actor leaning against the back of a barstool.

"A whiskey, dry. And a cranberry-vodka. Please." I wait for our drinks, trying to be subtle as I pinpoint who the actor is. Then he catches me looking, and I divert my gaze to the liquor bottles on the top shelf behind the bar. Too late. He walks over.

Once he's closer, his name pops into my head. Nolan Aries. Of course.

"Olivia, right?" he says.

It's so weird having these people know who *I* am.

"Yeah, and you're Nolan?" I shake his extended hand.

"I saw your TV spot you did for the YOUTHelp Foundation. Good work, but sorry I put you in that situation. I was stuck in New York."

"That's what Nat—" I about choke on my words. My drink's ready and I take a quick sip, trying to act casual. "That's what Natalia had said." Just saying her name, even her fake name, makes me want to vomit. "You had meetings or something?"

"Always." He laughs and asks the bartender for a beer. "I'll let you get back to your evening. Just wanted to introduce myself. The foundation is important to me, so maybe we'll have a chance to work together in the future."

"That would be great. See you around." I take my drinks and walk back to Devon, handing him his and settling in next to him again.

"You hitting on movie stars now?" he asks, sarcasm dripping from his voice.

"Oh yeah. You know me." I'm really pleased with that interaction though. For one, I didn't come across as a total idiot. And, it was the first time I've gotten to talk to someone in a professional way. They claim Hollywood is all about connections. Well, so's the fate of my career, and it'll be great to have someone like Nolan in my network. "He was talking about YOUTHelp and working on projects in the future."

Devon rubs my back. "Sorry he brought it up. I know that whole thing is still bothering you."

What? No, I'm excited. Why would the foundation bother me? It wasn't the nonprofit's fault Nat attacked me. Or was it?

Is the foundation a fraud too?

My heart breaks a little at the idea. Now that the thought's crossed my mind, there's no un-thinking it. Would they really take advantage of me—of Jared—like that?

Oh man, I need to regroup. This is supposed to be a fun night.

"I'm going to run to the bathroom real quick, okay?"

He leans his head back against the couch. "I'll be here."

"Are you sure we don't need to leave? You look pale. What's wrong?"

There's the smirk again. What's the joke I must be missing?

"We'll talk when you get back. I'm okay. I promise."

We'll talk? Those are ominous words. I head to the bathroom with a million assumptions running through my head. No, we promised no more assumptions. We're honest with each other now. Everything's fine.

I push through the bathroom door and almost plow right into Lex.

"Sorry. There you are. I was wondering—"

I survey the scene in front of me. The women's bathroom opens to a small sitting area, the walls covered in mirrors for unlimited access to makeup touchups. The bathroom stalls and sinks are separated by a glass partitioned wall.

Lex is nearest the door, and another woman sits on one of the armchairs, a small vile in her hand.

"Hey Livi. Look! I just met Mara. She was an extra on that show Werewolf Chronicles. Cool, huh?"

This is the same girl who was critical of all of Hollywood earlier, but I can see the inspiration for her new opinion. A small tray sits on the table between them, and on that tray, a small line of coke waits.

I shake my head, "Really, Lex? You couldn't stay sober for one night?"

Mara laughs and Lex joins her. Screw it. I walk past them to the furthest stall with the intention of getting out of here as quick as possible. Forget my hopes for a fun night of sibling bonding. As I wash my hands and leave the bathroom, Lex starts to speak, but I let the door swing shut, cutting off her words.

Doesn't she get it? Hours ago, she describes her mother and everything they went through. And here she is, making the same mistakes? What the hell is it about these dumb drugs that people can't make rational choices?

I find Devon, and before considering my words, I say, "Your half-sister's snorting coke in the bathroom."

I don't know which makes me feel worse—my disregard for everything we've been through about drugs or the look of sheer hunger that crosses his face.

"I shouldn't have brought it up." I sit down next to him and comb my fingers through his hair. "Sorry. I wasn't even thinking."

"Want me to go stop her?"

Are you kidding? I don't want you anywhere near free drugs. "No, no. I just don't know what to do about her. How can she act like that after watching her own mother die from the same behavior?"

Devon's quiet, and I know he's taking this personally. He should. I saw the way he practically drooled when I told him what Lex is doing. It's so unbelievably frustrating that I can't get through to anyone, but I'm also not in the mood to fight.

I grab my drink from the coffee table in front of us and finish it off. This night's a bust. I pull out my phone and figure I can distract myself on that until it's time to leave.

Ten missed calls.

Five unread text messages.

"Devon, something's wrong with Maddie."

I swipe across the phone's screen, hurrying to get to the texts.

I need to talk to you.

Answer your phone.

O, this is an emergency.

I need you.

The fucking bar caught on fire.

CHAPTER EIGHT

My heart sinks and I jump up. "We have to go. Now."

"What is it?"

"There was a fire at Maddie's work."

He follows me out of the VIP room and we stop by the bathroom to grab Lex.

I grab her arm and yank her away from her new friend, Mara. "We're leaving."

She resists, but she's too high to do much about it. "I'm staying," she says, her speech excited and hurried. "I want to dance and get up on the stage and—"

"Come on," I say again, this time with force, and she pouts as she follows behind.

Keeping my grip on her, we wade through the sea of dancing bodies until we're out front again. Devon's got Mark on the phone and he's pulling around now.

He hangs up and looks down at me, genuine concern on his face. "Is she okay?"

"She didn't say." I try calling her but it goes to voicemail this time. "She just left a bunch of messages."

Mark pulls up and we pile in. I tell him to go to Brecken's Sports Pub.

Fifteen minutes later, we pull up to a hectic scene. I'm already a nervous wreck, but seeing all the police tape and fire trucks and smoke still billowing up from the bar's roof, a real panic sets in. Where's Maddie?!

Devon and I get out, but Lex is curled up on one of the seats with no intention of leaving the limo. That's one good thing that's happened tonight. At least she won't be out here causing a scene or getting into trouble.

We're barely halfway through the parking lot when I hear, "Olivia!"

Maddie's standing next to an ambulance with a blanket wrapped around her and an EMT checking her vitals.

"Oh my god, Maddie. I'm so sorry I didn't see my phone sooner." I throw my arms around her, disregarding the medic trying to work. "Are you okay? What happened? Was anyone hurt?"

Maddie's makeup is smeared like she'd been crying. "Everyone got out. They said it was started in the kitchen. Someone dropped a towel on the grill or something, but this night's been...weird." She looks at the EMT. "Can I go?"

He nods an approval. Maddie tosses the blanket in the back of the ambulance, grabs her purse, and we walk back toward the limo—which, by the way, looks horribly out of place next to all the emergency vehicles. We get back in, this time with Maddie. She gives Lex a quick glance and looks at me, eyebrows furrowed.

"Don't ask," I tell her. Lex isn't a priority right now. "Are you really okay?"

"Not really. I think the bar's destroyed. That's why the whole thing doesn't seem right."

Devon pours Maddie a shot of whiskey, but I intervene. "She might need to give a statement or something."

Maddie takes the glass and swallows it all in one gulp. Never mind.

"How does a towel, accidentally catching on fire on the grill, lead to the entire interior of my workplace being scorched?"

"No one was around to witness it?" I suggest.

Maddie shakes her head no. "We had staff back there. They extinguished the towel really fast. But there was something on the floor—all over the floor. That's what ignited the whole place."

"So grease? Oil? What?"

She shrugs her shoulders. "I don't know. We're really particular about keeping the floors clean. We just had an inspection. It doesn't make sense unless..."

Devon finishes the thought with a tone of amusement in his voice. "...It wasn't an accident." He says it like he's doing a suspenseful voiceover.

Maddie glares at him. "Exactly, smart ass."

Devon straightens up. Only he can find a way to joke right now. "So who hates your boss? A disgruntled employee?"

"Funny you should ask." Maddie pulls out her phone and shows us a message. "I got this right before it all happened."

A text message that includes a photo, just like what Nat sent me the other day at the Stone mansion. It's a photo of the bar taken earlier tonight, I assume. And the message:

Have a nice night.

"You know who sent this," Maddie says to me. "Just like she sent the message to you. She's trying to threaten us—all of us."

The look on Devon's face is one of hate and fury. "She? Natasha? She's messaged you?"

"Hey," Lex speaks up from her side of the limo. "Is she the reason your car crashed today?"

And now I have three sets of eyes on me, waiting.

I avoid eye contact with Devon as I come clean about everything. After showing him my text from Nat, I tell him about the flowers that had been waiting for me in my room.

"I thought she was just being creepy. It's not like a message or a bouquet would kill me. And if she wanted to kill me," I think back to waking up in that maintenance closet, "she already had the chance." And would she? Would she go so far as to *kill* for Devon?

"That photo," Devon points to Maddie's phone, "is proof she did this." He motions out the window to the bar. "But why? She doesn't even know Maddie."

"No, but..." The message Maddie left Nat plays back through my head. "Maddie called and threatened her, telling her not to mess with me anymore. I think it made her mad."

"You think?" He looks to Maddie. "How very bold of you. And what was that about your car?" We all check on Lex who seems to be asleep. Granted, I hadn't thought she was listening in a few minutes ago either.

"The mechanic called me earlier. Said the accident didn't appear to be an... accident. My brake lines were punctured."

"And you told Lex but not me?"

I can't tell if he's angrier at me or the crazy woman who did all these things to us.

"No. She was in the car when the brakes went out. I didn't tell her what they found out with my car. That was just a good guess on her part."

Devon glares at me as he tries to process it all.

"I'm sorry I didn't talk to you about all this right when it happened. It didn't seem like a big deal until my mechanic called, and by then, my priority was on you and Lex and—"

"Don't do that. You really think us going out to some club—where she could've been, by the way. Did you consider that? Did you really think that was more important than telling me you're getting threats from her?"

It sounds ridiculous when he says it out loud. "I was going to talk to you about it in the morning."

Devon sighs and pulls out his phone. "Mark, take us to Olivia's." We start down the street, and Devon makes a phone call. "You need to find Natasha ... Mhmm .... She's at it again, this time going after Olivia ... I want her in cuffs. She violated the restraining order, attempted homicide, and committed arson. I want the highest charges pressed. Got it? ... Call me back once you have her." He hangs up, watching out the window, not looking me in the eye. "I'm staying with you tonight. My guys will find her."

"The same guys who didn't find out about Lex before we did? Are you sure—"

"They'll find her. I want you to stay out of it. And I'm the first to know next time. Got it?"

Devon ditched his button-down shirt and is lounging in my bed wearing only his jeans. This view of him makes me forget all my troubles. Maddie's asleep. Lex is passed out on the couch. It's just me and Devon, and I have him all to myself. Staring at me as I climb into bed next to him, he hardly flinches when I lean over him and kiss his collarbone.

I move down to his chest, trailing kisses past his nipple and down his stomach. When I reach the top of his pants, I trace my finger along his skin, drawing an invisible line from one hip bone to the other. His muscles are hard, his body warm. Ready for me to consume him.

Unbuttoning his pants, I look up at him, unable to keep a flirty smile off my face.

"Can you not?"

My mood instantly deflates, and I fall back onto the pillow next to him.

"I told you I was sorry, okay? I didn't know she'd take it that far, and—"

"It's not that. That's done with. She'll be found and arrested."

I prop myself up on an elbow facing him. He takes my free hand and holds it in his.

"Why do you think forcing a relationship between me and Lex is so important? More important than your life being threatened?" he asks.

"I lost the only sibling I had. And I know you have Kaidan, but...who does she have? She's in a bad place, and I feel like we're the only ones who can help her." *And I'm the only one who can help you.*

"She's an adult."

"She's your sister, and it's more obvious by the minute." My hand rests against his chest, and I try to focus on his heartbeat rather than how hard it is to let the truth come out.

"What's that supposed to mean?"

I can't help him if I can't be open about everything, right? "She's a drug addict. She doesn't consider anyone else when all she wants is to get high. Her entire life is a mess because of it."

"So you think she's another version of me? That my life is a mess?"

"No...yes...I don't know. I watch her, and it scares me. Last week, you showed up here in the same state I've had to see Lex in. I believe in us. I think what we have matters. And I wish you felt the same. I wish you'd see yourself the way I see you and just *try* to get better—to get help."

Devon closes his eyes, and I'm afraid I'm annoying him rather than reaching out and letting him know my honest feelings.

Then he laughs. Now I'm confused.

"Migraines, uncontrollable shaking, constant exhaustion, feeling like shit. Yeah, I'm not trying. That's why I'm fucking going through withdrawal." He opens his eyes and looks at me, a mix of sadness and sincerity in them. "I'm doing it for you. For *us*."

"I had no idea." I lay my head on his chest, feeling like a jerk. He isn't just sick. He's not using. Did he get rid of his stash? That stupid little tin box?

Instead of interrogating him, I let his confession fill the room with a new hope. How do I support him through this? Just trust him to take care of himself on his own? That doesn't seem fair. Just because it's his battle—

No, it's our battle.

CHAPTER NINE

"Where'd Devon go?"

Maddie and I sit in the living room, feeling about as useless as we can with this whole Nat ordeal.

"He went to meet up with his security guys. The ones who are supposed to be catching Nat. Between you and me, I doubt their competence."

She laughs, and the bathroom door opens to reveal Lex. She's wearing nothing but her black tank top and underwear, but she has something in her hand. Her pants lay on the floor by the couch she's been sleeping on, and she tucks her mystery item into one of the pockets while sniffing loudly and repeatedly. Without a word to us, she collapses onto the other couch and stares at the spinning ceiling fan.

Maddie and I give each other a frustrated glare. It's not like Lex is good at concealing her drug use, and now we get to watch her doped-up antics while we twiddle our thumbs.

"You know what's bothering me?" I ask the room.

Maddie's eyes go wide as though she expects me to tell off Lex, but that's not it at all.

"Nat got to me through the YOUTHelp Foundation. How can somebody so awful be a part of something so beneficial? And if the foundation is a fake, that means everyone else who works there is just as bad..."

It's sickening to think about it—that they'd exploit real victims for their own pleasure.

"Then let's find out." Maddie stands up. "Devon's off doing his part. We can do ours."

With everything Devon's going through? I don't want to do anything to upset him, and he asked me to stay out of it. "I can't. I agreed I wouldn't go after Nat."

"Who said anything about her? No, we have every right to check on the foundation itself. Who's that woman in charge of it?"

"Rhyanne?"

"Yeah, her. Let's go have a chat with her."

An hour later, Maddie and I are sitting across from the founder herself. Rhyanne Phoenix had been so kind when I met her at the gala. It had seemed like the foundation really mattered to her. I don't know what I'll do if she knew the truth about Nat all along.

"You have an employee here, Natalia Vorhees."

"I do," Rhyanne beams. "She's one of my newer assistants, but she's fabulous. Why do you ask?"

I try to speak, but choke on my own words.

Maddie does it for me. "Her real name is Natasha, and she's certifiably insane."

Rhyanne laughs.

Oh no, she does know the truth. I can't handle this.

"I'm sorry, girls. Maybe you should start over. Why are you here?" Rhyanne leans back in her chair. I look around at the walls and shelves covered in awards, certificates, and photos from charity events.

I find my voice this time. "Natasha has a restraining order against her due to stalking charges from a couple years ago. She's been following me to get to Devon Stone. After the gala, she...she attacked me. She knocked me unconscious, and when Devon found out what happened, she fled. Since then, she's sent threatening messages, she caused me to wreck my car, and she set her workplace on fire." I point to Maddie. "I know this sounds crazy, but I can show you proof."

And I do. I show her the messages, play the voicemail from the mechanic, and I pull up a news article about the fire at Brecken's.

"But this doesn't make sense," Rhyanne says. Her voice is quieter, and she holds her hand to her mouth. "This doesn't sound like the girl I hired at all."

"She had me fooled too. And she's really clever. There were a handful of times she was in the same place as Devon, and if he'd seen her for even a second, none of this would've happened. But she's sneaky and puts on a believable act. All the trouble she went through just to get me to the gala, making me believe my brother's death mattered—"

"Oh honey. His death *does* matter. Don't doubt that for one second. Natalia may be leading a deceptive double life, but the rest of us? This foundation? We're here to make sure *you* know what happened to your brother matters."

I can't stop the tears once they start. An enormous weight lifts as I hear her speak.

"When we hire people here, we go through a thorough review. We've had several in the past try to bring us down from the inside. There are awful people out there who don't agree with our values or who have a problem with social equality or a problem with," she smiles, "me. I thought we'd found a foolproof application process, but I guess not. It's a shame, but maybe there's a bright side."

"Like what?"

"Like...we have a charity party tomorrow night. Natalia's been one of the head coordinators, which means there's no reason she won't be attending."

What sort of stealthy, investigative scheme is this? Rhyanne gives us the details where and when the party is taking place. It's a celebrity thing, so we have to be careful to not bring attention to ourselves. But if we can be discreet, we can catch Nat.

Sounds like we have a plan.

"I specifically asked you not to do anything. How can I keep you safe if you keep intentionally putting yourself out there?" Devon paces through the living room.

Maddie and I are both amped up now that we have information that can put an end to all this. Unfortunately, Devon doesn't share our enthusiasm, and Lex...Well, Lex found a second to put her pants on while we were gone, but she's still camped out on the couch as though there's nothing else to do with her life.

Oh well, her issues are on the back burner for now. We have a solution to the Nat problem, and I'm not letting Devon talk us out of it.

"It's safe, and it's a guarantee. Have your guys found her yet? Because you'd think it wouldn't be that hard, but apparently she's smart enough to live a double life without getting caught."

Devon thinks for a second, stopping his manic pacing and running his hands through his hair. "It's not a guarantee. She's been watching us. She'll see you coming. She'll see me coming."

"Then we call the police. We tell them everything and have them go pick her up."

Devon laughs, shaking his head. "No way in hell am I making this a public spectacle. My guys can keep it discreet. The LAPD? The media would know in a heartbeat. The Stone family doesn't need more scandal."

"I'll do it."

We all turn to the sound of her voice. Lex, lounging on the couch, is watching us with interest.

"Right," Devon says, "and all this can come down to us relying on you? No thanks. Tell me, when was your last hit? Judging by the glazed look in your eyes and your slow speech, it's probably about time for another line, right—to amp you back up?"

"Apparently, you know as well as I do. But you said you need help. I'll help."

Before Devon berates her, I stand up. "It's okay, Lex. We can take care of this."

"Whatever," she says, her voice lacking inflection. Does she think this is all a game? "She's not watching me though, that chick you're talking about. Unless she's been staring through that window." She points to the window next to the front door.

"She's got a point," I tell Devon. "We have proof she's been following me and you and Maddie. But Lex. No one knows Lex."

"You're right. *We* hardly know Lex. She's unreliable. She'll fuck everything up."

Lex gets up and storms out of the apartment.

I glare at Devon. "Come on. I get you're angry about us going to Rhyanne, but don't take it out on her."

"It's not about that," he says through clenched teeth.

And then I get it.

He's trying to give up drugs, and Lex is...She's the mirror version of him if he wasn't stopping.

Devon retreats to my room, and I follow.

"You want to get out of here?" I ask him. "I know it can't help you to be around Lex, especially when she's..." I won't point it out. He knows.

"She can help. I guess it's our best option." He laughs at how ridiculous this is—that the most unstable of us all is our best bet. "But after, she's got to get out of here. I'm going to lose my damn mind if I have to be that close to...you know."

It's become the darkness we cannot speak of. Is that a healthy way to get clean?

"We'll talk to her after tomorrow. One thing at a time, alright?"

CHAPTER TEN

"Tell me the plan one more time," Devon demands.

All four of us are piled in the back of the black Escalade that belongs to Devon's security detail. His two guards sit up front waiting for our cue. Outside, the hotel across the street is crowded with a line of cars waiting for valet, a red carpet lined with media, and groups of fans waiting to see their favorite celebrities. My heart pounds in my chest. This is it.

It's all up to Lex who's getting more defensive every time Devon speaks to her. "I know the plan. I'm not an infant."

She's dressed in the red Calypso Day gown Maddie was given. Her hair is styled and smoothed with spray, and she wears a simple gold necklace around her neck. The only one in heels, she swears she can pull this stunt off without tripping. All we need is for her to act natural.

"Amuse me." Devon glares at her until she gives in.

"Fine. I'm heading toward the red carpet. I've got the cell in my purse, and you'll be on speakerphone. The woman on the..." She squints out the window, making sure she has the details right. "The one on the left with the clipboard. Rhyanne told her to expect me. So I go to her. Give her the name Alexandria Rogue, and she'll let me in through the staff entrance. From there, I find your crazy stalker-lady, I follow her without her noticing, and once she's somewhere easily accessible and discreet, I give the secret code to unleash the guards."

"There's no secret code, Lex." Devon won't take a joke to save his life right now.

"I think there should be one. This is like some action movie or something. There should *definitely* be a secret code." She thinks for a second. "The donut shop is open."

"The what?" Maddie asks. "That's far more suspicious than, *We're ready. Come and get her.*"

"I don't know," Lex says. "I'm hungry. But now we have our secret code."

Devon shakes his head, irritated. "Just get out there."

She double checks to make sure the phone she has—Devon's—is connected to the one we have—mine. All that's left to do is cross our fingers and hope this works.

Lex opens the door and climbs out as I whisper a good luck. Once the door's closed behind her, Maddie, Devon, and I glue our eyes to the window, watching Lex until she's lost in the crowd.

I nervously tap my fingers against Devon's leg, waiting for her to say something. So far, the only noise we hear is the muffled sounds of the crowd and a shuffling from the phone being pressed against the inside of her clutch.

I'm still tapping my fingers, when Devon's hand slides over mine and squeezes. "Everything's fine. Calm down."

But I can't. This is really it. If we fail...how will Nat retaliate? "What if it doesn't work? She came after Maddie over a voicemail. What will she do to us over this?"

"Don't worry about that right now."

I raise my eyebrows. Does he know who he just told not to worry?

"How about this," I offer. "I'll stop worrying if you agree that if this all goes wrong, we contact the police."

"You know I don't want—"

"And I don't want to wake up to a stalker hovering over me with a knife."

Devon sighs. "Fine. I'll consider talking about *maybe* going to the police, but only—"

"...Alexandria Rogue..." we hear from the phone. Lex is using some ridiculous fake accent. We all freeze and stare at the phone sitting in my lap.

"Right this way," a woman says.

"She's going in." I know, I know. *Miss Obvious,* here. I bite my lip and listen. *Focus, O.*

More shuffling, and then we hear Lex say, "Thank you, darling. I've got it from here." Only, because of her stupid accent, it sounds like, "Thank you, dahhhling..."

Then a loud scuffling noise makes us all cringe before we hear, "Hey. You guys there? I'm in."

She's going to blow her cover in two seconds.

"Great," I say. "But we need you to not be so suspicious."

"What are you talking about?" The accent's back. "Right now, I'm a very important Hollywood star taking a very important phone call." *Vahry impwahtant phu-one call,* it sounds like.

Devon pinches the bridge of his nose, and Maddie giggles.

"Just find what we're looking for, Lex," Devon pleads.

"Say what? I don't understand that code. Try again."

Devon looks up and clenches a fist like he's going to punch the phone.

I throw my hand up to wave him off and tell Lex, "Find the damn donut, okay?"

"On it," she says with a cheery voice. "This place is all decked out. Can I stop at the bar first?"

"No!" we all yell in unison.

"You guys are so boring. Alright," she lowers her voice. "Judging by the photo Devon showed me off the old police report, I'm looking for a hot Russian chick. Dark hair... Oh wait. I think I see her. Just a sec."

We here movement, and then my phone beeps.

"Did she just text you?" Maddie asks.

And she has. She's just sent us a photo. *She took a photo of Nat.*

"Is this her?" Lex asks.

"Yes, but what the hell are you doing?" I can't believe how bad she is at this. "You can't go snapping pictures of her. Be discreet. *Discreet!*"

"You can see for yourself she wasn't looking at me. Chill out."

None of us speak. She needs to stick to the plan. It's only a matter of minutes before Nat will have gone somewhere less obvious. And at that point, we can step in and take care of the rest.

An eternity seems to pass with Lex offering occasional commentary about which celebrities are walking in and what food's being served. We keep reminding her to stay quiet, and finally she gets it and puts the phone back in her purse.

Relief washes over us all now that she can easily blend in with the guests. And about two minutes later, we hear her on the move.

"This could be it," I say, again stating the obvious.

We sit up straighter, anticipating our cue.

More shuffling.

A strange yelping noise.

Something falling.

My eyes go wide. Something's not right about this unless, maybe, Lex just dropped her purse in the toilet or threw it across the room.

"Shit guys. The donuts aren't cooking!" Lex yells.

"What the hell does that mean?" Devon's voice has that sexy powerful tone to it, but this is no time to admire my boyfriend.

"The donuts have left the bakery."

"What are you saying, Lex. Dammit. Where's Nat?" I can't take the games anymore.

"She's gone. She just shoved me into Ethan Beckham and ran. I can't say I'm mad though. He's hot."

We jump out of the SUV as though we've found a bomb. The guards get out with us.

"She ran," Devon tells them. "We can't let her leave."

CHAPTER ELEVEN

We can't race into the party and cause a scene. Instead, we walk around the side and push through to the staff entrance, ignoring the woman with the clipboard demanding we stop.

"You and Maddie stay near the doors. The guys and I will split up and search. Be careful, okay?" He kisses me hard before running down a hallway.

"We can't just stand here. He knows that right?" Maddie surveys the main floor of the hotel. "If we split up, one of us can check the rooms down here. And one can go upstairs."

"And one of us can check outside." Lex has found us and is ready with new ideas.

I'm not sure we can afford to have her help more, but what else can we do?

"Fine," I say. "Lex goes outside, Maddie upstairs, and I'll search down here." I pat at my pockets and pull out my phone. "Call me if you find her. Do whatever it takes to stop her. Just," I look around at the well-dressed guests who are completely clueless to what's happening, "try not to cause a scene."

We rush off our respective ways. The guys each took a hallway, so I start with the kitchen. Chefs and servers eye me suspiciously as I search under counters and in the walk-in pantry. That crazy bitch can be anywhere. But she's not here. I go back out and check in closets and offices.

"Can we help you?" a check-in receptionist asks.

"I'm fine." And I don't need to be interrupted. I slam the door open for the women's bathroom and check in each of the stalls. It's empty.

"I need to see your credentials." The receptionist is following behind me, growing more impatient by the second. "All the staff tonight's required to have a name tag. Security reasons."

I stop and stare at her. "I can't deal with you right now. Everything's fine, but...but this is important. Go back to your desk and make it look like everything's normal, okay?"

She does, but on her way to the desk, she calls to the other receptionist. "Pearl, I need you to call security. I think we have a problem."

Dammit! I need to hurry and get out of the lobby. Party guests are still arriving in their gowns and excessive diamonds. As they work their way back to the ballroom, a few notice me but merely raise an eyebrow. I clearly look out of place wearing jeans, and the curiosity in their glances is as though they're wondering whether or not I'm *really* Olivia Margot or just some ordinary woman who looks like her. Great. Tonight, let me pass for ordinary. It'll make things easier.

On the other side of the lobby, I push open the door for the men's bathroom.

It's not empty. Ethan Beckham stands at a urinal...doing his business.

"What the hell?" he shouts.

I ignore him, checking the room as fast as possible, my cheeks burning with embarrassment now.

As I leave, Ethan mutters under his breath. "What the hell is wrong with this fucking place tonight?"

Oh right, Lex said she was shoved into him by Nat. Sorry Ethan. Tonight's just not your night.

Back in the lobby, two hotel security guards wait at the check-in desk, getting details from the receptionists.

Shit.

I hide myself in the crowd, hoping they don't notice me, and race down the first hall that gets me out of view.

My phone's buzzing in my pocket. I yank it out. It's Maddie.

"She was up here! Took the stairs." Maddie talks in bursts, gasping to catch her breath. "Knows we're here ... Coming your way."

At that exact moment, a door swings open, and Nat comes out looking like a frightened deer. We lock eyes for a moment.

And then she runs.

This time, all efforts at being discreet are a waste. I shove my phone back in my pocket and race after her, pumping my legs faster than I've run in years. Nat disappears in the sea of incoming guests, but I push through them, trying not to think about *who* I'm pushing out of the way.

Sorry Bia. Sorry witch from Werewolf Chronicles. Sorry guy in that one band I can't remember.

I push through them, running toward the door. A second of clear space reveals Nat, exiting the main door.

She *can't* get past the media line. The blockade set up means she only has one way out—the red carpet.

I get through the door only a few feet behind her.

Nat tries to run faster but gets caught up in Ender Varrone, and the rest of Cylon Smash, taking up all the space on the red carpet. If I reached out with my arms, she'd only be inches away.

But if I jump...

I can't believe I'm going to do this.

Nat gets past the band, who stays out of the way for me. Thank you, gentlemen.

Then I do it.

On the fucking red carpet. In front of cameras. In front of the entertainment reporters. In front of the tabloid journalists.

Pushing into the plush red carpet. I leap forward. I reach out—determined.

And I land right on top of her.

I bring the bitch down.

And just as quick, the hotel security guys are on me, pulling me up.

"Don't let her go!" I yell. Flashes from all the cameras blind me, but I'm focused on Nat. Please don't let these idiots let her get away.

"Are you alright, miss?" they ask Nat.

"No, she's not alright. She tried to kill me. She tried to kill my best friend. She—" I feel the cold metal of cuffs close around my wrists. "What are you doing? No. She's the one you need to cuff. Believe me." I plead with them, but it's no use. The guard holding onto Nat's arm will let go any second, and when he does, she'll run.

My chest heaves as I try to catch my breath and figure a way out of this. Reporters are yelling questions at me.

"Olivia Margot, what is going on?!"

"Olivia, are you drunk?"

"Olivia, why is your life going downhill?"

"Olivia, where's Devon?"

I can imagine the headlines already.

The guard holding me looks from one of the reporters to me, his face clearly confused. "Let's go over here and let these folks enjoy their evening."

Nat and I are led to the side of the building near the staff entrance. The red carpet resumes its parade of top celebrities and party guests, but half the media has followed us to get more story.

"What's happened here tonight?" the guard asks me.

The other one, with piqued interest, keeps his hold on Nat to ensure his role here is still important enough to stick around.

"This was the only way to catch her," I say, breathless and near tears. Nat is right in front of me. We have her. "You can't let her go," I tell the guard holding Nat. "She's in a lot of trouble. She's a criminal and—"

Nat bursts out laughing. "Oh, Olivia. You're hilarious." She looks at each of the guards, her eyes bright and flirty. "We used to work with each other. It was all about pranks with her. This might be her best one yet. You can let her go. It's just a game we play."

"It's not. I swear."

"And who are you exactly?" the guard asks.

"Olivia Margot."

The guard looks to the reporters. "And you're what? An actress? A—"

"No. I'm—"

Devon races out the staff door, Maddie, Lex, and the private guards following behind him.

Thank you, thank you, thank you. I can't help but smile. "I'm with him."

Now the attention is on Devon and everyone around us is going wild. The media are fighting to ask questions first. The flood of camera flashes illuminates the entire scene. And Nat's immediately taken into custody by one of Devon's men.

"Get those things off her." Devon points to the handcuffs on my wrists, and the hotel guard does as he's told. "We have this taken care of if you can secure the area and get them," he points to the paparazzi and reporters, "back where they belong.

Tears stream down my face and adrenaline rushes through my veins. I throw myself into Devon's arms, eternally grateful that we pulled this off. I'll deal with the mortification of it all later. For now, we have Nat. We did it.

Once the cameras are out of our faces, Devon steps closer to Nat.

She flutters her eyelashes. "Hi baby. It's nice to see you here."

"You're going to listen to me very carefully," He inches his face closer, dead serious. "You're going to be arrested now and then charged with the highest counts my lawyers can prosecute you with. You will be locked up for a very. Long. Time. And if the day comes when you get to see sunlight again and walk the L.A. streets, you will not come anywhere near me, my family, or anyone I know. And—

hear me very clearly now—you will not even *think* about Olivia. If I find out you so much as speak her name, I will have you taken care of. These guys here..." he looks at both his guards, "they can get rid of people. No questions asked."

Devon stands up straighter while my heart tries to burst from my ribcage. He just gave her a death threat, and judging by the looks on his guards' faces, it might not be a threat at all. It's a promise.

"Get her out of here," Devon says, and Nat is led off to the Escalade.

As quickly as she disappears out of sight, a limo pulls up, the window rolls down, and we see Mark.

"You guys ready to go?"

Just like that—it's over.

CHAPTER TWELVE

While we got one problem out of the way, one more still exists—Lex. Well, one and a half, if I'm being honest.

"I can't help but feel like it's my fault you're out of a job," I tell Maddie.

She's hanging out with me while I nervously wait for Devon and Lex to come back from an errand. Really, that's all the information I got. "We're running an errand." And then they left.

"It's no big deal. I liked working at Brecken's, but it's bartending. It's not like there's a shortage of bars around here."

Still, I can tell she's not happy. "Do you want to talk about anything? You seem down."

Maddie switches from her couch to the one I'm sitting on and leans her head on my shoulder. "I feel like you've come a really long way in the past few weeks. I'm sure Devon's a part of that reason, but I'm so proud of you for finding your confidence and staying true to yourself. You have so much greatness ahead of you."

"Thank you." The compliments are nice, but... "What's wrong?"

"In, like, a month, you've made all these self-discoveries and you've grown and things are looking better for you by the day. Meanwhile, what do I have? I feel like my life is stagnant. My job was destroyed. My love life is nonexistent. I don't even know who I am or who I want to be."

We sit in silence for a moment while I think of the right words to say. "I couldn't be who I am without you. You're the greatest friend anyone could ask for. You encouraged me. Believed in me. And you saw things in me and Devon that we couldn't see. I know things are rough right now, but I'm certain it will get better for you. You know? This time next year, who knows where our lives will be. If I've learned anything, so much can change in such a short time."

She laughs. "For real. One day, you're afraid to leave the apartment. The next, you're tackling stalkers on the red carpet."

I feel my cheeks warm. I *cannot* believe it came down to that. This morning, we all laughed at the *ScandalLust* headlines:

"Never Mind Who She's Wearing On the Red Carpet, Who's She Whacking?"
"What's With The Fists of Fury, Devon's Girly?"
"Olivia Margot Has Lost Her Mind—And in Those Shoes?"

"How did this become my life?" Haven't I always said I wanted things simple? And what did I get? A Devon Stone.

We both jump as the front door opens. In walk Devon and Lex, their arms filled with bags from boutiques and expensive department stores.

My jaw drops. This day just got instantly stranger.

"Did you two go shopping?" Maddie asks. "And you didn't bring us?"

Devon grins, then turns to Lex. "Why don't you get ready in Olivia's room."

She nods, and they disappear to my room. A minute later, Devon comes back out, his arms empty. He sits down across from us, resting his arms on his knees as though he's about to give us a pep talk.

"We're going for a ride today." He's looking at me, his face intent and serious. Then he lowers his voice even more. "There's a place a couple hours up the coast. Luz Del Sol. It's a ninety-day rehab facility. I convinced Lex it's time for her to check-in. We made a deal. If she can clean herself up, I'll help her get settled here. Help her find a job, a place to stay. But she has to complete the program."

"Good," I say, trying to hold back a massive grin. I wasn't sure how he'd act after yesterday's ordeal. He had sounded so set on ditching her, but she'd helped us—no matter how awfully she did it. She'd been there when she didn't need to be. Now it's our turn. "So she's packing? You guys went shopping to get her stuff?"

Devon leans back and relaxes a little. "Yeah. I mean, she's a Stone—sort of. She needs to look the part and since she came here with nothing...But the real reason I took her, I figured it would make it easier for her to handle the severity of the compromise. This treatment facility, it's a really good one. You only get one shot though. You voluntarily check yourself in, but then they control you. You don't get to come and go. You don't get visitors. Your phone calls and mail are monitored. If anyone can treat her, it's them, but once they approve her for check-out, she's on her own. It's up to her to stay clean. And if she doesn't, if she screws up and needs help again, they won't take her back. I needed her to understand that before she agreed to it."

Wow. It's obvious this is important to him. He wants to see her succeed, and it makes sense. She's the last piece he has of his mother. Through Lex, Devon will find his own closure. Since he never got the chance to be there for his mom—to try and help her clean up—it's like he's determined to do so with his sister.

I move over to his couch and lean into him, my head resting on his chest. "You're a good person. What you're doing for her...it's the greatest gift she'll ever receive."

Devon kisses the top of my head. "Let's just hope she takes it seriously."

It takes all afternoon to finish getting Lex ready and to make the drive up. The ride in

Devon's Camaro is mostly silent. Lex, in the backseat, seems understandably nervous. Will she go through with it? I'll make sure we encourage her as much as we can, but, she's only just become a part of our lives. How much do our opinions matter?

She's an adult. She'll figure it out for herself. We all have to be given room to grow. And when the right people support you, the options are limitless. Hopefully, she'll recognize that too, and when I see her in a few months, she'll be a new, better version of herself.

When we pull up to Luz Del Sol, I'm blown away by its beauty. I'm not sure what I would've expected from a rehabilitation facility, but this place...this place looks like a luxury resort. It's surrounded by trees, and being near the coast, there's a steady breeze bringing everything to life.

We get out of the car and stand near the trunk. It's quiet out, only the sounds of rustling leaves and birds to escort you to the wooden doors of the facility.

Should I hug Lex? Tell her how proud I am of her? Will it make a difference?

She's quiet, but I sense something in her— hope, determination?

Oh what the hell? I wrap my arms around her, pulling her into a hug. "You're going to do great." I pull back and see she looks equally surprised and grateful. "I know we're not exactly friends, but I'm here for you, okay?"

Lex nods. "I hope we're friends in ninety days. I like you."

I smile and look to Devon. He should give her a hug or something. Come on, big brother.

He fidgets with the keys in his hand like he's thinking of what to say. I'm sure Lex just wants to hear any words of encouragement— no matter how silly they may sound.

"Well, this is it. You ready?" he asks her.

"If I say no, are we driving all the way back down?"

"Nope." Devon puts his arm around her shoulders and squeezes. "It's now or never."

"Then *now* it is."

Devon turns and opens his trunk, pulling out Lex's brand new designer suitcase. He sets it down next to her and she takes the handle.

My heart thumps quickly with excitement. No matter how challenging the next couple months will be, I'm happy for the promise of her future—a much brighter one than her mother's.

Then Devon reaches into his trunk and pulls out a second bag, his duffel. He slams the trunk shut and turns to me, not quite looking me in the eye. My throat catches.

"What's going on?" I ask. No, I plead. What did I miss?

"I'm checking in too." He drops the duffel bag on the ground by his feet and takes my hands in his. "You know why."

My hands tremble, my stomach feels hollow. It's hard to breathe. "Why—why are you telling me this now? You can't just drop this news and leave me like this."

He smiles his sexy half grin, his icy blue eyes on me. I can't stop the tears that blur my vision. I don't know whether to feel thankful that he's finally getting help too—after all these years of addiction—or hurt that he kept this plan from me.

"You'll be fine," he says. "*We'll* be fine."

Will we? Our relationship is so new. What happens when we don't see each other for months? As he gets better, will he still have the same feelings for me? What if he changes his mind? Or worse, what if the rehab doesn't work? What happens then?

There are too many what ifs. Too much uncertainty.

Devon wraps me in his arms and kisses me softly. "I know it scares you. That's why I didn't give you more time to worry. But I promise, everything will be okay."

"How can you be so sure?" My voice quivers, and I feel panic enveloping me.

"Because I have you. And you have me. And I'll do whatever it takes to hold onto the girl I've fallen in love with."

All the panic dissipates with his words. He's the one who makes me feel whole, who makes me feel *normal*. Can we make it through this? We *have* to.

Devon kisses me one last time and places his keys in my hand. The keys to his beloved car. The car he doesn't let anyone drive.

"Take care of it. Please." He smiles and I return the same happy, hopeful expression. "I'll see you in ninety days."

And with that, they walk toward the entrance to Luz Del Sol. I hug my arms and breathe in deeply, gathering my own strength while I watch them disappear. Devon and Lex. Brother and sister. Supporting each other in a way Jared and I never got to.

With only the sounds of nature surrounding me now, I look up at the bright blue sky. Everything's uncertain. But there's so much promise. Devon, Lex, Maddie, even myself.

We're all going to emerge from the darkness.

90 DAYS LATER

The rumble of Devon's Camaro sends birds scattering as I pull up to Luz Del Sol on this exciting Friday afternoon. Those who know me understand I can sometimes be an anxious mess. But even those closest to me would be shocked by this level of nervousness.

I haven't seen Devon in ninety days. Some might laugh. After all, plenty of people manage long-distance relationships all over the world. But still, it's been difficult, and in ninety days, life feels so much different than it did three months ago when I left Devon and

Lex here. We've gotten to talk, thankfully, but our conversations have been supervised. It's not like we've gotten to divulge private thoughts or engage in phone sex. Instead, we'd talk about day-to-day topics: the weather, my new job, updates on Stone label artists. We sent each other mail, little love letters that reminded me of being a teenager again. I have all four of his letters tucked in an old memory box I keep in my closet. But even those had to be written knowing someone besides him and I would be reading them. I guess they were afraid people outside the facility would try to ruin all the progress that's been made or that those in rehab would try to reach out to their drug dealers. I don't know. All I know is each conversation and letter felt charged with trapped electricity, and today...today I get to see him again.

I can't ignore the subtle disappointment that Lex isn't coming home with us, but according to Devon, she's doing better. She just needs a little more time.

Waiting in the car, I fidget with my phone. *ScandalLust* has had fun creating rumors about us.

"Devon and Olivia No More? Did OliVon Fizzle Out Already?"

"Olivia Margot Heartbroken—Devon's Been Seeing Four Other Women!"

"Olivia Who? Devon's Former Girlfriend Returns to 'Nobody Status'"

And I don't bother to correct it. These assumptions have allowed us both a certain degree of privacy. No one in the media knows Devon's here, and I'm no longer harassed by pirate-impersonating paparazzi. That'll change soon enough when we're seen together, and then the rumors will change.

This'll be our life. And I'm completely happy with that.

From the corner of my eye, there's movement, and I snap my head up in time to see the door of the facility open. Devon walks out, his bag slung over his shoulder.

Forget trying to keep it all together, I let the tears ruin my makeup as I jump out of the car and run straight into his arms. He wraps me into a hug and then pulls my face up to kiss me. His lips, soft and sweet, graze mine until he crushes into me, kissing me with force. My breath catches, and a familiar tingle runs down my spine. My body on fire, I tangle my fingers in his hair and hold tight to him.

When we break free, I stumble over all the words I want to say. "I'm so happy to...You're out...How are you feeling...How's Lex...Do you—"

"I love you." He stares down at me, and I feel my knees go weak.

A laugh escapes me. Here I am, an emotional, nervous wreck. And here's Devon, sure, confident, and very much to the point.

"I love you too."

He kisses me again, this time lifting me off the ground. Then he leans in close to my ear. I breathe in the scent of him as he whispers, "Let's get the hell out of here."

I hand over his keys and we walk back to the car hand-in-hand. He holds the passenger door for me, then goes around to his side, tossing his bag onto the backseat. He settles into the driver's seat and leans forward, planting a big kiss on his steering wheel. "I've missed you too," he tells his car.

Ninety days worth of what ifs fly out the window as I look at Devon, how happy he seems, and accept that this beautiful life is all mine.

It's a long drive, but I'm loving every second catching up with Devon.

"How's work?" he asks me.

After Nat was arrested, Rhyanne Phoenix and I talked a bunch. She still felt bad she didn't know about Nat's double life. But with her in prison, it left a job opening at the YOUTHelp Foundation. Take that, crazy stalker bitch. I got rid of her *and* took her job. "I love it," I tell Devon. "It's everything I wanted in a career. I get to work with amazing people and do work that really matters. I can see myself staying with them forever."

"Maybe you'll take over as President of it someday."

"Maybe." I smile at the thought. "Maddie got a new job too. It's another bartending job, but she's happy with the money."

"That's good. Kaidan said the Stone name is finally free of all the scandals that had been piling up. It's been good for the label and the law firm."

"And which do you want to return to?" I ask. We limited all talk of the Stone family while he was in rehab, but I know he's been considering his professional future with his family.

"I'm not sure yet. I'll go back to doing the grunt work I'd been doing—tracking down new artists, working for the firm as needed. We'll see which one I like more now that I'm sober." He laughs, but it's really not a joke. Things'll be different for him now that he doesn't have his old vice to turn to. But I have faith that he wants to stay clean.

"Did you hear from Kaidan often?" I ask. He'd made it clear Devon needed help, so I hope he offered support.

"Yeah, Lex and I both got a chance to talk to him. It's been especially good for them, now that he knows she's really his half-sister and that she's not so bad. He's been really encouraging. I think it's because of his girlfriend."

"Why's that?" I'd seen plenty of Kaidan and Hayley Wade in the papers. Apparently, they've been in Paris, vacationing.

"He's never been this happy with a woman. He's got a messy past when it comes to love, but Hayley seems to keep him grounded. It's funny. Whoever thought the troublemaking Stone twins would find the only women on this planet who can keep them in line?"

"You think that's true?" I eye him carefully. If our ninety days apart have made anything clear, it's that I really do love this man.

It's crazy how our lives were thrown together, and now, I can never imagine us apart.

"I know it's true," he says, taking my hand and kissing the back of it. "Love'll do that to a person."

"Hmm. *ScandalLust* will be disappointed then."

Devon looks over, his eyebrow raised.

"They're going to kick you off their Lust List."

Just when I think we're getting closer to home, Devon takes us on a detour. Not that I'm against more adventures, but right now, more than anything, I want to be home with him, curled up in bed. Preferably naked.

"Where are we going?"

"You'll see," is all he says.

A few minutes later, he pulls up to a security gate at a condominium called The Promenade. He uses a key card to get in, and we stop at the valet.

"Welcome, Mr. Stone," the valet driver says, holding the door for me.

Devon comes around and offers me his arm. "I have a surprise for you."

This must be another one of his secret lairs. I want to roll my eyes, but at the same time, I'm giddy with excitement. How many ways will he surprise me throughout our relationship? All the secrets he's kept from others, how long will it take before he tells me all of them? We've got years of discovery and understanding ahead of us as we learn more about each other. Have I mentioned how much I love this man—and love my life?

Devon leads us inside and uses his key card at the elevator to take us to the top floor. The doors open to reveal a quiet hallway with giant windows that show off the slowly setting sun. Still gripping my hand, Devon leads us to a door with 802 displayed in metal numbers.

Standing behind me, Devon kisses the back of my shoulder. "Ready?"

"For what?"

He unlocks the door, and we go inside.

A mostly empty living room awaits. The entire back wall is lined with windows with an incredible view of the Pacific Ocean. To the right, a modern kitchen and empty countertops. A small dining room is off to the side, a round table and chairs already in place under an industrial looking iron chandelier. The floors are a dark wood. And in the living room, they're covered with an enormous, plush, white rug splayed before a marble fireplace.

On the rug, there's a flower pot with a great, big white orchid plant, and next to it, a little card propped up.

I look at Devon, who's watching me for a reaction. "What is all this?" I ask.

He just smiles. I drop my purse onto the kitchen counter and go to the card, stooping down to pick it up and read it.

Will you make a home with me?

My heart leaps, and a warmth floods through me. I'm so used to him turning me on or making me feel crazy, but this, this feeling is one I'll always hold sacred. Love.

Before I can get up, he's at my side. I press my lips against him and push him down onto the rug. Running my tongue along his bottom lip, I comb my fingers through his hair and settle my hands against his firm chest. Breathless, I pick my head up and look at him.

"You *are* my home, Devon Stone."

"So you'll move in with me?"

I sit up straight, giving him room to get up. "How did you do this? This place looks brand new."

"I had ninety days in rehab to think about what I really wanted. I want you. One of the therapists there is married to a realtor. He got me in touch with her, and she helped me find this place. She played the middleman between me and the owners—and then me and the designers. I know it's sparse right now. That's because I wanted you to help. I want this place to be yours—*ours.*"

He bought us a condo. How do you top that?

"Can I see the rest?"

"That depends. Will you live with me?"

I smile and kiss him again. "This became our home the second we walked in."

He pulls me to standing and leads me through the rest of the place. A big master suite is furnished with a king size bed covered in pillows. The floor-to-ceiling windows continue in here, and I'm already looking forward to all the mornings I'll wake up to the view of the ocean.

We check out the master bathroom, the guest suite, and the back balcony.

"This place is breathtaking. Thank you." I look out at the water and take in the night breeze. The sun's getting lower and the sky's a beautiful gradient of oranges and purples.

Devon stands behind me, his arms wrapped around my front. "I thought of you when I bought it. I didn't want it to be too big—something cozy and simple."

I laugh. "It's both bigger and more extraordinary than anything I'd ever expect to
own, but it's amazing."

"You know my favorite part?"

"Hmm?" I turn around to face him, loving
how the light of dusk makes him look even
sexier.

"This balcony. The privacy of it, yet it's
out in the open."

I look around and notice both sides are solid walls. The neighbors can't see in. And
we're much too high up for beach-goers to see
us with the half wall that blocks the view of
the ground. All we can see is the shore and
the horizon and the colorful panorama of the
sky.

"It *is* pretty private, huh?"

Thinking fast, I turn us just enough to line
up Devon with the upholstered lounge chair
sitting behind him. I push him down onto it,
and straddle him. I wore a dress today, so the
limited amount of fabric from my panties
makes the feeling of him beneath me over-

whelmingly pleasurable. I grind into him, encouraged as he moans.

"Fuck, I missed you," he says, his voice hoarse and low.

His hands grip my hips, and I lean down to kiss him. Our mouths are hungry from all the days we've been without each other. Sucking on his bottom lip, Devon grunts and pushes me down onto him harder. I'm wet and eager and reach down to unbutton his jeans. These have got to go!

I stand up, well aware that I'm outside, and usually I'd be too shy, too self-conscious to do this. But those feelings are nowhere to be found. I tug my dress over my head and watch Devon as he takes in my half-naked body. I'm down to my bra, my lacy panties, and a pair of white heels. Then I ditch the bra, and, finally, the panties. I'll keep the heels on. It's kind of sexy.

Leaning down, I take off Devon's shoes, his socks, his shirt, his jeans—tossing each to the side. With each article of clothing disappearing, my body responds more intensely. I'm on fire and need him, now. And he, very obviously, feels the same.

"One second," I say, and hurry inside. I practically sprint to my purse, digging inside for the condom I'd grabbed for this exact opportunity. I knew we'd both be eager to jump on each other, but I never expected it to be *here*.

Outside, I finish what I started and strip Devon of his boxers. He sees the condom and grins. "I love a girl who comes prepared."

"*A* girl?" I ask playfully.

"*My* girl." He puts the condom on and pulls my body down onto him, not wasting any time.

I cry out at the sudden penetration, but it feels so good, and I was more than ready. We've missed this, the choreography of our bodies as we find our rhythm and violate each other in the best ways.

My gaze drifts over his broad chest, and I watch as the muscles in his arms tense each time I come down onto him. The way he stares at me makes me melt—his eyes fiercely focused on me, as if there's a chance I'll disappear if he looks away. He seems mesmerized by the movement of my body, slow and sensual, and he smiles lazily when I moan.

Clenching my muscles, I can feel the length of him massaging me from the inside, and the pleasure of it is too intense. Picking up speed, the first convulsion runs through me, and Devon feels it too, because he bucks his hips hard, hitting me deeper.

With each thrust, my body screams with ecstasy. Devon lifts his head to kiss my mouth, my neck, my shoulder. Hungry for more, he nibbles and sucks at my breasts, my nipples, and back up to my collarbone, my ear. I ride him harder and faster until we reach our peak. My body comes unbound, and Devon growls in my ear as we both climax. I keep grinding into him, the intensity unbearable, until we're both completely spent, and then I collapse onto his chest, both of us fighting for breath.

Our erratic heartbeats drum together, and a thin layer of sweat makes both of our bodies shine. The sun's been replaced by the moon, and it feels like this entire world only exists for the two of us.

I shiver from the open air on my exposed skin, and Devon reaches to a nearby table, revealing a storage space under the top. He pulls out a small throw blanket and wraps it over me.

"I love a man who comes prepared." My voice sounds sleepy, but I have no intention of getting up and going to our new bedroom. In fact, I don't plan on falling asleep. As soon as I find the energy, I'm beginning round two with my naked Devon.

Devon squeezes me and clears his throat. "*A* man," he asks with the same playful tone I had before.

I laugh. "*My* man."

I roll over so I can stare up at the twinkling stars above us. With Devon embracing my satisfied body, and lying here in the comfort of our new home, one thing is clearer than the gorgeous night sky:

Everything is perfect.

FOUR LETTERS

Jump back in time for the prequel series that gives glimpses into Devon Stone's past—the life he lived before Olivia came along.

The Lust List: Miles Riot follows music journalist, Abby, as she's stuck touring with the rowdy rock band, Tempest Ultra.

While the series occurs on a timeline before *The Lust List: Devon Stone*, it can be enjoyed and read in either order.

The entire series is available now!

THE LUST LIST

The Lust List - Take Your Pick
They're the world's sexiest bachelors. The men of *ScandalLust* mag's infamous Lust List are young, wealthy, and, oh, did we mention? *Hot.*

When scandal follows them everywhere, there's no hiding from the cameras. They're irresistible, insatiable—and talented in all the right ways. Every woman wants them. But these playboys won't be easy to catch...

THE LUST LIST
DEVON STONE

by MIRA BAILEE

FIRST TASTE
SECOND CHANCES
THIRD DEGREE
FOUR LETTERS

Acknowledgments

This is the fourth and final book in a series I would never have been able to complete without you, my readers.

It's your enthusiasm and excitement for each installment of The Lust List: Devon Stone that made my fingers type faster and my creativity run wilder.

I can't wait to bring you more from the Lust List world, and I assure you, *Scandal-Lust* will have more drama to report and more sexy men to exploit in the future. Until then, LIVE, LOVE, LUST.

Thank you.

About Mira Bailee

Mira Bailee, a beer-brewing librarian, has been writing leisurely, scholarly, and professionally for the past twenty years.

While she's always maintained a high standard of chaos in her daily routine, *The Lust List* allows her to pass on some of her hectic lifestyle to her characters. Her storytelling balances humor and pleasure with sincerity and conflict, providing a wild ride of human emotions.

In the past she studied filmmaking and screenwriting and determined what goes on behind the scenes is just as tantalizing as what's seen in front of the camera. This revelation is the basis for her inspiration for *The Lust List.*

Made in the USA
Columbia, SC
26 January 2024